HYPERPHOBIA

DREAMLAND

Two Performance Art Plays

Charles Serio

St. DeSales, London 2023

St. DeSales First Edition 2023
978-1-9996159-4-9(Print)
978-1-9996159-5-6 (e-Book)

Copyright©2023
Charles Serio

Cover Art: Roger Fletcher

HYPERPHOBIA

Charles Serio

ORIGINAL CAST AND CREDITS

Written and directed by: Charles Serio
Designed by: Mari Cardew Richardson, Alan Maye,
and John Pettenuzzo
Choreography: Karin Trembeth
Projections: Anders Gramer
Costumier: Camilla Bak Olesen
Make-up: Karoline Skovgaard
Hairstyling: David Larcombe
Lighting: Dan Watkins
PA Music: Alex Hughes

PLAYERS:

Idoia Aristegui
Jean Buckland
Adrienne Celli
Lukie Gramer
Alex Hughes
Jonquil
Karen Lennon
Allan Lochhead
Meri Pakarinen
Karin Trembeth
Julian Shaw
William Simpson
Malin Skoglund

MUSICIANS:

Graeme Selkirk, Korus, Gyan, J. Owen Williams, and
others

HYPERPHOBIA premiered in London at The Pigeon Loft Theatre, June 1998.

HYPERPHOBIA is a mixed performance arts piece of roughly five hours in duration. It combines elements of theatre, music, dance, and media arts. This piece is structured into sections focusing on different performance arts. There is live music performed occasionally throughout the evening. At the conclusion of each music set, a theatre or dance performance takes place. For the purposes of this performance arts piece, the script has been broken down into five sections. Each section follows a live music set of roughly twenty to thirty minutes in duration. In the original production, there was no live music break between Sections Four and Five.

SET
The setting consists of a 'stream of mirrors' which winds its way through the venue floor and separates the seating area from the live performance area. Access to the performance area is made via a bridge over the mirrored stream from which the performers enter and exit. The audience is seated at tables and chairs that dot the periphery of the stream. There is a large central platform across the bridge on which the theatre/dance sections take place. The central platform is flanked, right and left, by two large screens suitable for back projection. Images are projected on to the screens to suggest locale and mood for each theatre or dance performance section. In the original production, an additional smaller platform served to house the Live Music sections and other divertissements throughout the evening.

Performance Art Section 1

FX: Lights 'Divertissement' area-First Music Section
PA Music is followed by Live Music #1. At the conclusion of this first music set…
FX: Crossfade lights to Central Platform

An elderly couple (**Players #1 and # 2**) cross the bridge to the Central Platform. They walk hand in hand. When they arrive at the Central Platform, they speak directly to the audience.

PLAYER #1

My fear is churches. I do not like them. I even have nightmares about them. Nothing will stop me from being frightened by them. Especially at night. Or worse when you do not know that they're there and just stumble across them. Gee willikers! It gives me the creeps. And that's the truth.

PLAYER #2

Dolls. God, they scare me! They terrify me. I hate dolls. Especially the eyes. Also tailors' mannequins and ventriloquist dummies. They are like evil. I mean, really. They send a shiver right through me just thinking about them. Cor Blimey!
(**PLAYERS #1 and #2** exit across the bridge)

FX: Lights on Central Platform fade with exit.
FX: Images up on projection screens for 'Lonely Girl' monologue.

PLAYER #3 enters as images are projected and takes her place on the Central Platform.
FX: Lights up/ Central Platform

'LONELY GIRL'

PLAYER #3
(Addressing the audience.)

I was so frightened of people that I just wanted to die.
I just wanted to fade away, disappear down the rabbit
hole, and be no more. To un-exist.

It all started when I left primary school and lost touch
with all my friends. My father was in the navy and we
were always moving about. I didn't have a 'normal'
home like most kids. At secondary school, in yet
another new place, I changed. Teachers, classmates,
neighbours- I began to fear everyone. It was like they
were all staring at me, because they knew I did not
belong there. Especially boys. I always felt like I was
being sized-up. I was always afraid of making a fool
of myself. I felt like an alien. Like everything was
foreign and unknown to me. I kept imagining that
everyone was talking about me behind my back. I was
so self-conscious that it was actually painful. I had no
self-confidence at all. It affected my appearance. My
shoulders started to stoop. I walked everywhere with
my head bowed low and never ever looked anyone in
the eye. Even when they spoke to me.

Then my dad was transferred yet again and my life
became impossible. I was sent to a new school where
the boys were in one building and we girls in another.
I'd do anything to avoid walking past the boys'
building. And when I had no choice but to walk by,
the boys would start shouting ugly things at me from
out the window.

I just would grit my teeth, put my hands over my ears, and hurry by as quickly as I could while they stood there laughing at me.

I'd purposefully arrive late to school every day and then run across the vacant schoolyard to use the back entrance to avoid the other students. I'd even make myself ill, if there was some school event. I dreaded school assemblies. I started to wish that I was invisible or, better still, that I had never been born at all.

Walking in the street was a nightmare. I'd wait on the opposite side of the road, if my bus stop was crowded with people. The only time I could relax at all was when I was on my own. If my father asked me to go out to fetch him some cigarettes or something, I'd make an excuse why I couldn't go. He thought that I was being 'difficult'. How could I tell him that I was terrified to go to the corner shop?

At sixth form, I kept completely to myself. If anyone spoke to me, I'd blush a deep scarlet. I never saw a single classmate outside of school. In fact, I never saw anyone. I'd just stay in my room listening to music or reading. I lived in my own world. I knew the only person who could help me was me, but I was too crippled inside to do anything about it.

Eventually, I managed to get a job in an office through my dad's friend. There was no way that I could have gone through an interview. There were only six of us working there, but it took me forever to settle in.

I trembled with fear whenever the phone rang. I jumped whenever someone walked by me. I'd sit in my little back office all day long pretending to be happy there. But inside? I was totally lonely and depressed.

I remember that I used to daydream about exciting things that I'd like to do, but I gave up hope of ever having any of them come true. How could they? I was scared of everyone. You see, I had convinced myself that I was just stupid, dumb, and ignorant-a real nobody. I felt trapped, locked inside myself. It was awful. Everyone made me feel jittery. I thought, 'I can't live like this'. Not for another moment. I longed for the end of me. Then I'd be free.

Then one day, a miracle happened. There was an office party and even though I was petrified the entire week before, I plucked up enough courage to go. One of the new men in the office came over and started talking to me. At first, my face went all red, but he was so kind and friendly that I started to relax in his company. Then it just happened. I started telling him about everything. I told him how lonely I was, about how I thought I was a nobody, and I couldn't take it anymore. Don't you see? I had never confessed that to anyone! And there I was pouring my heart out. It helped me so much. Just to have someone listen and not telling me how silly I was. He just smiled and listened. I think he really understood. We never went out or anything. I don't think that I am capable of having a relationship. But that night, talking with him, was a real breakthrough for me.

Although I still often shake like a leaf inside, I can hide it much better now. I can answer the phone without my heart in my mouth. I don't go all red-faced nearly so often now. I can even laugh and joke with my co-workers.

My behaviour has really improved. I look people in the eye when I speak to them and my speech which used to be so rapid and stuttery is much slower and precise. I still don't go out much and I've never had a boyfriend, but it doesn't worry me so much anymore.

My advice to anyone out there with the same problem is to try and talk with someone. Anyone. It doesn't have to be a professional. It's the opening up of what you are hiding that matters. I know it's hard, but people might be more sympathetic than you think. Like my White Knight at that office party. You never know. After all, I never dreamed that I could tell my story aloud to all of you tonight. But I did, didn't I? And I didn't blush! Not even once! (Exit)

FX: Lights/blackout
FX: Projection images out for 'Lonely Girl'

Phobic couple (**PLAYER #1/PLAYER #2**) reenter and cross to the Central Platform.

FX: Lights/ Central Platform

PLAYER #2
Don't even think about touching my neck! I can't bear it. I even scream when my husband does it. Don't I, dear? And this is not funny! Do not touch my neck!

PLAYER #1
Everything is too heavy. Especially buildings and lorries. The ground just can't possibly hold the weight. Can't you see? Even when I'm having a bath, I think the bathtub is far too heavy and I will go crashing through the floor. Why doesn't anyone understand this? (Exeunt)

FX: Lights cross fade to 'Divertissement' area.
FX: Sound affect of water running in a sink
FX: Projection of a bathroom sink

SOLO PHOBIC PERFORMANCE #1
(Mysophobia-fear of germs) A **PLAYER,** yet to be seen, mimes washing and rewashing their hands over and over again. They repeat in a stage whisper throughout, "Germs! Can't scrub them away! Can't wash them away!"

FX: Lights in Divertissement area fade to black.
FX: Projection out
FX: Sound effect out.

FX: Projections for 'Stage Fright', suggestive of a therapist's office, appear on the projection screens.

PLAYERS #4 and #5 cross to Central Platform

FX: Lights/ Central Platform

'STAGE FRIGHT'

A Scandinavian woman, **Mary**, **PLAYER #4**, enters the Central Platform. She is wearing pyjamas and speaks with a slight accent.

A **Doctor**, **PLAYER #5**, sits behind an empty desk. There is a second chair facing the desk.

MARY
Hello. My name's Mary. I'm an actress.

DOCTOR
Sit down please. (He mimes answering a ringing phone.) Not just now, Alice. I'm with a patient. (He mimes replacing the receiver) Pardon me, Mary.

MARY
It was very difficult for me to come here. I don't like doctors.

DOCTOR
Neither do I.

MARY
But you are a doctor, aren't you?

DOCTOR
Yes, you can call me Bill.

MARY
Hello, Bill

DOCTOR
Hello, Mary

MARY
I'll be late for my call time at the theatre, but I don't care. I had to see you.

DOCTOR
Why? What's the problem?

MARY
I need help. Help me. I am desperate. Can you help me?

DOCTOR
I'll do my best.

MARY
Cure me, Doctor. I'm terrorized! … I don't like sitting (She stands). This chair is too tight. I can't breathe.

DOCTOR
Make yourself comfortable.

MARY
And maybe you can turn down the lights. They hurt my eyes.

DOCTOR
Of course
(He mimes dimming the lights)

FX: Lights dimmed/Central Platform

DOCTOR
Better?

MARY
Muchly. 'Tack'.
(Or another foreign expression of 'thank you').

DOCTOR
You were saying?

MARY
Pardon?

DOCTOR
You're terrorized?

MARY
Yes! I'm shaking all over. The fog, the food, the foreigners! Oh, it's all too much. I don't like fog. You can't see through it, you know? It makes everything… foggy. And bubble baths. I used to love my bubble baths. Now I don't like them either. "Clear water, clear sailing", that's my new motto… And the food! You can't trust the food anymore, can you? No matter how much they say it's safe… Well, you know, don't you?

DOCTOR
It isn't safe?

MARY
That's funny. (She giggles.) That is funny.

DOCTOR
What is?

MARY
Acting as if you didn't know! Of course, the food
isn't safe. Everyone knows the food isn't safe. It's
just common knowledge.

DOCTOR
Is it? Everyone knows it?

MARY
Yes. Certainly they do. They all just pretend it's safe.
The cowards… I don't. I know.

DOCTOR
The food isn't safe.

MARY
Exactly

DOCTOR
The fog, the food, and the 'foreigners', you said.

MARY
Yes, yes, yes! They're everywhere. Tourists. Peruvian
buskers. Americans with their loud voices and
Harrods bags. It's all so awful. There's no escaping
them. You can't avoid them.

DOCTOR
But aren't you foreign yourself?

MARY

Yes, but that's not the point, is it? The point is you
can't escape them. I'm alone. They hunt in packs-
their tour buses, crowding the museums. I'm alone. I
make very sure that I don't bother anyone.

DOCTOR

You're alone?

MARY

And I don't make myself a nuisance.

DOCTOR

I see.

MARY

And I need help. What's happening to me? I can't go
out. I can't stay at home. I have to work. I can't eat. I
can't sleep. And it has been so foggy. So dreary
lately. The misty rain. It's unhealthy. Everyone's ill.
Coughing. Sneezing. I can't go on public transport.
Everyone hacking all over me. It's an epidemic. I
can't walk. The foreigners stare at me through the
windows of their tour bus. The charity muggers
accost me on the street. My eyes are cloudy. I can't
see. I'm exhausted. I don't know if I am awake or
asleep.

DOCTOR

Perhaps that explains why you are wearing pyjamas.

MARY

Pyjamas?

DOCTOR
Your pyjamas

MARY
What about them? Don't you like them? They're very
expensive pyjamas, I promise you.

DOCTOR
Yes, I like them. They are lovely pyjamas. It's only
wearing them at my surgery, I…

MARY
Of course! Let me explain. I am wearing these
pyjamas, because I am working on a role.

DOCTOR
An acting role?

MARY
Yes. I am playing a character who can't sleep. She
has a sleep disorder. She's a bit of an eccentric. I'm
wearing pyjamas to help me get under her skin.

DOCTOR
Well, that explains it.

MARY
So you see, you really must help me. I have a
performance to do. I have a responsibility. People are
depending on me. It's all very difficult in my current
condition. Perhaps there's a pill I could take? Or
some shock treatment? Perhaps I need shock therapy.

DOCTOR
I don't think that would be wise.

MARY
Yes, it would. Snap me out of this! Let me eat and sleep and go out again. I can't stand this. Not for another single, solitary moment. Do it now. Please!

DOCTOR
It might come to that. But perhaps we should start at the beginning. When did this all start? How long has this been going on?

MARY
When did it start?

DOCTOR
Yes, start at the beginning.

MARY
Let's see… I suppose it all began about the time I was cast in this role.

DOCTOR
As the woman who can't sleep?

MARY
Yes. Her. She mustn't sleep.

DOCTOR
Right. Tell me about her.

MARY

Well, she came to this country to get away from some very painful memories. She is haunted by a dream. Years ago, she lost her daughter. She drowned. Every time she fell asleep, she kept having the same dream about her.

DOCTOR

What sort of dream?

MARY

It's quite frightening really. Petrifying. She dreams that she is drowning too. She is underwater and she sees her little girl swim by. But she can never reach her.

Then, the 'Queen of the Sea' appears. The 'Queen of the Sea' tries to trap her there. She grabs her and won't let go. She is drowning her in her sleep.

DOCTOR

The Queen of the Sea?

MARY

Yes. So she's afraid to sleep now. And she moves here to try to escape her dream.

She thinks, if she can get away from where it all happened, the dreams might stop.

DOCTOR

And do they?

MARY

No. The drowning dream has followed her here.

DOCTOR

That could be significant.

MARY

Why? Do you think this might have something to do
with my problem?

DOCTOR

I think it might. It sounds as if you are identifying
with your character very strongly. Very likely, your
role is causing you to suffer sympathetic anxiety. You
are, so to speak, taking your work home with you.
Avoid working on your role just before bedtime.

I recommend some soothing chamomile tea, a hot
bath (no bubbles), followed by a good night's sleep.
We'll forget about the shock therapy for now, shall
we? I believe your anxiety will dissipate once you
leave this character behind.

MARY

Yes, that is so. I am identifying with her.

DOCTOR

And you transfer her anxiety to yourself in the form
of these phobias and paranoia.

MARY

And they will disappear as easily as that?

DOCTOR
Very likely. If not, come back and see me.

MARY
Thank you, Bill!

DOCTOR
I hope that I've helped. When does your show open?

MARY
Tonight

FX: Lights-Blackout on Central Platform
FX: Projections out for 'Stage Fright'

Performance Art Section 2

FX: PA music as necessary for Live Music #2 set-up.
FX: PA music out/ lights up in 'Divertissement' area.
Live Music #2
FX: At end of set, lights crossfade to Central
Platform.

Phobic Couple (**PLAYERS #1, #2**)
Cross the bridge and enter the Central Platform

PLAYER #1
I'll never drive. That's for sure. It's even difficult for
me to walk. You see, I have a phobia about traffic
lights.

PLAYER #1
(Continuing)

When I approach one, I go into a panic. I can't move one foot in front of the other. I can only walk when I know I won't see a traffic light enroute. Full stop.

PLAYER #2

I can't look in a mirror. I'm fine until I see my reflection. People say I look fine, but it's not that.

Any reflective surface will set me off. I think, "Who's that stranger?" Then, I realize it's me! That can't be me! That can't be me!
(They run off in a panic together.)

FX: Lights out/ Central Platform.
FX: Projections up for 'Phobic Dance #1'.
Dancers in position on Central Platform.
FX: Lights and sound for 'Phobic Dance #1'

PHOBIC DANCE #1- Ornithophobia
In the original production, a dance was choreographed expressing a fear of birds, ornithophobia. As the production premiered at The Pigeon Loft Theater, a fear of pigeons was the focus.

At conclusion of 'Phobic Dance #1'…
FX: Lights/sound out
FX: 'Phobic Dance #1' projections out

FX: Projections up for 'High Flyer'
PLAYER #6 enters the Central Platform
FX: Lights/Central Platform

FX: PA Music for 'High Flyer'- 'Come Fly With Me'.

HIGH FLYER

As lights come up, **PLAYER #1** reenters. Pretending to be a plane, he zooms around **PLAYER #6** while laughing at him. **PLAYER #1** then 'flies off'. (Exit)

FX: PA music out

PLAYER #6
(Directly addressing the audience)
I know you'll think I am being ridiculous. Don't worry. I expect this reaction. Everyone thinks so. I even think so. But I'm absolutely terrified of flying.

I shiver all over just thinking about flying.
I have tried and tried to overcome it. I've read the statistics. I KNOW it's safe, but I still FEEL it isn't.
Oh! The stories I could tell you.

Once, I hid for two days at Heathrow airport rather than catch my flight to New York. And that flight was for work. If I didn't go, I'd lose my job.
Eventually, the police found me hiding behind the desk at the lost luggage counter. I had to confess my fear of flying, so they didn't arrest me.

The following morning, I got as far as boarding the plane. But the next thing I remember was waking up in hospital. I had passed out in the aisle, so they told me. I was completely ashamed of myself.

I consider myself to be a reasonable person. I don't think I am bonkers. But at one stage, things grew so bad that I would run indoors whenever a plane even flew overhead.

I think it all began when I was only a wee tot. My mum took me on a small plane to visit my dad. It was terribly windy and the plane kept dipping and banking. I thought it was going to disintegrate. My stomach was doing somersaults. Even my mum was scared stiff.

I didn't fly again until I went on a school trip to Rome. I didn't think a thing about it beforehand. But during the takeoff, I started to feel all funny. As we gathered speed, an awful wave of panic washed through me.

I kept seeing all the other passengers as puppets. There they all were strapped down in their seats with no control over their destiny.

Then it suddenly hit me that I was a puppet too. Every time the jet changed speed or altitude, my heart would be in my mouth and I would shout out loud with fear. My classmates, of course, thought this was hilarious. But I just couldn't help myself.

Flying home, we were confronted by thick fog as we made our approach and all the planes at the airport had been grounded. The pilot's voice came over the tannoy to tell us that we were now cleared to land and he was going take us down.

Several times we swooped through the murk and then rose up again above it. We circled round and round going up and down like a yo-yo. The plane vibrated and shook uncontrollably every time we ploughed through the fog. And we had to land, because the fuel situation was growing desperate. Or so I imagined.

I started to think about how I could escape. Where could I go? There was no way out. I was trapped along with everyone else.

We dropped through the clouds once more and the plane was tossed around in the turbulence. I unfastened my seatbelt and jumped from my seat. I ignored the stewardesses telling me to sit down again and buckle up. I was like a madman, slobbering and crying, curled up in the aisle.

I was still lying there like that, when the plane finally did land with a bang and a bounce and the engines immediately reversed to slow the plane down. I thought the damn thing had blown up. I was not sure if I was alive or not.

It took three stewardesses and my headmaster to peel me up from the floor. But when I did get up and looked around, no one else was nervous or upset in the slightest. They were all acting like it was a great lark and applauded the pilot vociferously. "Wicked", someone said with a giggle. It was like a thrilling amusement park ride to them.

As for me? I was covered in sweat and shaking all over. Everyone teased me without mercy. They had no pity. After that, they took to calling me 'Ace'.

"How's it going? How's it flying, Ace?" And they'd stick their arms out to their side and pretend to be a plane dramatically crashing to the ground. This was all accompanied by gales of laughter. Believe me, that was doing nothing for my street-cred.

I've never been on a plane since. I've lost out on countless holidays, job opportunities, and my love-life has suffered too. My fear of flying has affected the quality of my life. Truly.

Even going to an airport to see off friends or family is an ordeal. I'll help them at the check-in desk and then shoot off as quickly as I can. I'd never watch them take off. Otherwise, my flying fears would run wild with all sorts of awful imaginings. Brrr! I can't bear to think about it.

As I say, I have read the statistics. Maybe it's my overly active imagination that creates these images of impending disaster and Doom's Day dread. Who knows?

But please don't tell me that flying is safer than being in a car or a train. Perhaps that's true, but it doesn't help a jot.

You know, in the old days they used to say if God had intended us to fly, He would have given us wings. And in a way, that's just about how I feel about it. Flying is for the birds.

PLAYER #1 re-enters and again imitates a flying a plane.

As he buzzes around the Central Platform, **PLAYER #6** soon copies him and they 'fly off' together. (Exeunt)

FX: Lights fade to black
FX: Reprise music 'Come Fly With Me'
FX: Projections out for 'High Flyer'

Phobic Couple, **Players #1 and #2,** enter from across the bridge and cross to the Central Platform

FX: Music 'Come Fly With Me' out
FX: Lights/Central Platform

PLAYER #2
My little girl is horrified by buttons.

We first noticed this, when she was just a baby. We go through tears and tantrums anytime she has to wear a buttoned garment. The poor dear!

PLAYER #1
Ships! Ships! Ships! If there's a disaster at sea and I see a photo of it, I just shut my eyes and squirm. A few months ago, a car firm used a ship in an advert. At breakfast, I was watching the telly the day they first aired it. I started choking on the toast I was chewing. I'm lucky to be alive.

(**PLAYERS #1, 2** exit hand-in-hand)

FX: Lights crossfade to 'Divertissement' area.
FX: Sound 'Mull of Kintyre'

FX: Screen Projection of bagpipes

SOLO PHOBIC PERFORMANCE #2
(Bagpipaphobia) A **PLAYER** paces up and down
with their hands over their ears as if in intolerable
pain. They continually repeat throughout in a stage
whisper, "Bagpipes! Lumpy and furry with tubes
sticking out! Bagpipes!"

FX: Lights in Divertissement area fade to black.
FX: Projection out
FX: Sound fades out

FX: Projections up for 'Snake Charmer'
PLAYER #7 crosses to Central Platform
FX: Lights/Central Platform

SNAKE CHARMER

Lights reveal a woman covered in snake tattoos. A
wooden box sits in front of her. The box has a top that
slides to open.

PLAYER #7
(Addressing the audience)

I'm going to tell you a story. It is a tale about my fear.
Well, more than that. I'm going to bear witness to you
this night. On this night, exactly one year ago to the
day, my brother passed on. I'm doing what I am
doing for you tonight as a tribute to him and to his
faith and my faith in him too.

25

You see, what I have here in this box is snakes. And I don't mind telling you that if you haven't got the faith, you better steer clear.

These are poison vipers. All sorts. They'd kill you as soon as looking at you, if they could. They have no hearts. They have no souls.

They are a slimy mess of wickedness wriggling on top and around the other.

And what I mean to prove to you-Right here-Right now-Right in front of your eyes- is just what true faith is all about. You see, you have to believe first, my friends. You have to know that there is a power beyond ourselves that is the source of all comfort and protection.

I reckon you won't believe me. I'm thinking you won't take my word on this. People, these days, they don't believe in nothing anymore, not even themselves, and so they get nothing in return. Like my brother said before he passed over, "If you don't believe in nothing, how can you expect something?" You get what you expect and believe in.

Oh! My brother! He had the faith. He knew he was protected. And one day at an outdoor revival, he showed his faith and stuck his hand in this here snake box. Yes, the one right here before your eyes. This very one.

I was there when it happened. I didn't want to be, but he made me watch.

He lifted his eyes to heaven, slid back the top, and plunged his hand in. He commenced singing a hymn with a smile in his face. He pulled out his hands a good five minutes later and he didn't have a scratch.

The halleluiahs from the crowd were deafening. And my brother stood up raised his arms to heaven, and said a silent prayer of thanksgiving. Now, that's faith. That's believing in an action of faith.

Later, he died when he was run over by a forklift truck down at the foundry. But that's different. That's not the point. We all of us pass on in the end.

But the point he wanted to show me, to show everyone, is the true power of faith. You see, he wanted to show all of us that real faith overcomes fear. Any fear.

And what I am here to do for you tonight is to prove to you what my brother proved to me. Believe! Believe and no harm ever will befall you.

Faith can move mountains, our sweet Lord said, and it can move you too.

Now, I suspect some of you are feeling queasy. Some of you may be a trifle uneasy. You don't want to think about someone as kind and cheerful and loving as myself sticking her hand in a mess of deadly snakes. Am I right? Of course I am. But at the same time, you all want to see me do it too.

We are all fascinated at the prospect of witnessing a true act of fearless faith. Such things help us to believe in some power greater than ourselves. Such witnessing will shake up our cozy or unhappy lives, put a spring back into our step, and let's us know-Yes! Praise be!-our future does matter. Our lives have a greater meaning than we imagined before. Because where there's faith, there is hope too.

For that, you will have to take my word for now. On that, you'll have to put your faith in me, brothers and sisters. God loves you. God needs you to believe to show His hand. It's His only need.

So, pray with me now, my friends, or keep a silent vigil, if you will. Right now! Believe along with me now! Hold your neighbour's hand. Raise your eyes and lift your arms up to the heavens. Lift them aloft!

FX: PA/Music cue

Feel along with me. Will me to escape the vipers' bite. Keep me safe in the bosom of your own concern.

PLAYER #7 begins to chant
Oo ma oo ma reema oh!

(**PLAYER #7** begins shaking and undulating to the music and her own chanting. Then silence.)

FX: PA/Music out

PLAYER #7

Damn ye old devil vipers! Damn your forkéd tongues
to the dark pit from which you crawled. The heavenly
cloak of protection is all around me! Let the divine
light…

FX: Light cue

PLAYER #7

Divine light spill upon me! Lift me up. Fortify me.
Bathe my soul. Look and believe with me, brothers
and sisters. I open this box! I open it now!

(**PLAYER #7** slides back the top of the snake box)

I thrust my hand into this box! I put my hand in now!
(She lifts her head and closes her eyes)
Crawl over me ye curséd vipers! Fear the power of
faith. You can do me no harm. I am here to bear
witness. I am not afraid for your glory is with me,
Lord! I am His faithful servant and you…you…you
are worms under His feet. You are the lowliest form
of creation. Eternally condemned to crawl on your
bellies.
(She suddenly looks down into the box)
You… you… you are…

(She shuts her eyes again and mumbles to herself, "I
am not afraid".
Then nervously, she begins to sing…)

(Singing)
♫ 'You are my sunshine
My only sunshine
You make me happy

When skies are grey
You'll never know, dear
How much I love you
Please don't take my sunshine away.' ♫

(**PLAYER #7** snapping out of her doubt)

No! There is no doubt! You are in my power! I command you in my brother's name to prove the power of faith to all the unbelievers.

Oh! Help me, Brother! Make me strong! I… I… I'm going to lift you vipers up! Raise you up in my hands! Show my people the power of faith!

(**PLAYER #7** puts her other hand into the snake box)

Lord God Almighty! Protect me!

(**PLAYER #7** lifts up 'snakes' from out of the box)

FX: Lights/blackout

PLAYER #7
(In the blackout)
Set me free!

FX: Projections for 'Snake Charmer' out

Performance Art Section 3

FX: PA music as necessary for Live Music #3 set-up.
FX: PA music out/ lights up in 'Divertissement' area.
Live Music #3

 At end of live music set, lights crossfade to
Central Platform.

Phobic Couple (**PLAYERS #1, #2**)
Cross the bridge and enter the Central Platform

PLAYER #1

I don't like matches. Or matchboxes either. Cigarette
lighters are all right, but matches and matchboxes fill
me with horror. I suppose this sounds loopy, but to
me, the idea of actually touching a box of matches is
revolting.

PLAYER #2

Since childhood, I've had a fear of homemade cakes,
biscuits, and pastries. Store bought, factory made
ones, they are fine.

I don't know why I feel this way. Maybe it's because
an old lady, who lived next door to us when I was
growing up, used to bake all the time. She had a
funny, old lady moustache. I think she was a witch.
(Exeunt)

FX: Lights out/Central Platform
FX: Projections up for 'Phobic Dance #2'
Dancers in position on Central Platform
FX: Lights/Central Platform and Music for 'Phobic
Dance #2'

PHOBIC DANCE #2-Coulrophobia

A dance piece choreographed to express a fear of clowns, coulrophobia.
In the original production, the dancers were costumed as clowns. A menacing dance spilled off the Central Platform and into the audience.

At conclusion of 'Phobic Dance #2'…

FX: Lights/music out
FX: 'Phobic Dance #2' projections out

FX: Projections up for 'Queen of the Sea'
FX: Sound effect- Sea Sounds

PLAYER #4 in position on Central Platform for 'Queen of the Sea'

FX: Lights/Central Platform
FX: Sound effect-Sea Sounds fade out

QUEEN OF THE SEA

A woman relates her story directly to the audience.
She struggles to stay awake throughout.

PLAYER #4
I had lived in that place all my life. I am not from here. I knew no one here. I came here to escape. To make my getaway.
(She suddenly shakes herself and shouts to herself.)
Wake Up!

Let me explain. Let me tell you my story while I still can. My tale begins in the early dawn at first light. It begins outside in the bracing dawn air.
Ah! The fresh air of the new day.
(She breathes in and out deeply.)

Early every morning, I'd walk along the seafront and watch the fishermen as they fumbled with their nets. I would scan the sky above them and watch the gulls treading the air and screaming their hunger at the fishermen below. But slowly, the cold and the damp would chill my bones and I'd find myself drawn back home. Back to my bed to warm by the fire. And very soon fall asleep again. And dream.

This had been my practice, my ritual, ever since she was taken from me. Ever since the sea had stolen her away from me. And left me bereft and abandoned. Alone. I would crawl back to bed, fall asleep, and dream. And in my dreams, I would see myself dreaming. Floating there above myself, when suddenly…Water! Water! I saw myself sinking. Flailing my arms to find the surface. I'm drowning! Drowning…

Then all is silence. I see myself drifting now, down and down, and smiling. As if drowning were a pleasant thing.
My head's swimming and full of wonders. I pretend I'm a sea creature searching for prey or an ocean explorer losing her way. I'm giggling! I'm singing songs in my head. Humming and watching the bubbles gurgling by. I snake myself deeper, drawn to the depths. Surveying my new water world.
(She shakes herself again)

Wake up! Wake up!... She fools me once again! She makes me believe that I happily go. Willingly go deeper and deeper. As if it were all my own idea to come to her lair. To come to her.

"Oh, spare me this dream!
Queen of the Sea
You've taken my daughter away from me.
Leave me to mourn in peace!"

But no. I dream on. She will not allow me to wake. She casts me in her dream spell. She holds me in a dream-prison cell.

And so stupidly grinning, I find myself on the seabed. Forever forgetting what awaits me. And then, I see her! My baby! My Marinna! I blubber out her name.

But she never stops. She never looks at me. She simply swims away with her hair trailing like the fins of an angelfish. She disappears from view as I clumsily try to keep up with her.

"Marinna!" I cry as she fades from view.
"Marinna!" But she's gone.

I feel myself tossing and turning. I know I am asleep, but I cannot awake. And fear grips me. I am so frightened. I can't escape my nightmare. I see myself thrashing about in the water, going nowhere.

I yearn to wake! And it is so cold there beneath the waves. The chill grips me. And it is growing dark.

I'm all alone. So dark!... What's that? There's a strange noise. I can't make it out. Who's there? I can't see.

"Who's there?!" I'm so frightened that I begin laughing hysterically. "Who's there? I know someone, something, is there! Who's there?!!!" Then slowly up above me, I see her descend. The Queen of the Sea. She is surrounded by her minions- all the little children she has stolen away and who now make their home at the bottom of the sea.

The sight of her is spine-chillingly majestic- all jellyfish and see-through. She seems to be made of the sea. She turns her blue-green eye and glares at me. So unnerving. Like the eye of the grave. So cold-blooded. Her bluish skin covers her like a shroud.

My frozen awe quickly turns to anger. "What have you done with my daughter? Bitch! Baby snatcher! Heartless drowner of the innocents!"

But she makes no response. Her silence is disdainful. Then with a wave of her royal watery hand, she signals to her entourage.

Soon, one, two of her consort brush up against me. Now three! More! No! They bump me and upend me. They're stealing the breath from me. They swarm and swarm about me. I feel my lungs fill with water. I cough and cough to get it out! No, no! I can't breathe. I struggle to get away from their teeming assault.

Somehow, I manage to wriggle free and swim away.
I swim and swim with all my strength, not daring to
look back. Wake up! Wake up! I must wake! But I
cannot.

I swim for the surface, but I make little progress. I
swim for my life. I'm drowning in my dream. She is
drowning me! She wants me too in her watery
graveyard. She wants me too! She wants me…

And suddenly, I am awake. I'm drenched in sweat.
My eyes are burning. I sit up and stare at the fire and I
have no idea how much time has passed.
(She shakes herself)
What time is it?!

From my window, I see the dawn's rising. I throw my
coat about me and head out to the seafront. To begin
my ritual again and walk in the cold, fresh air.
(She breathes in and out deeply)

I watch the fishermen fumble with their nets. I watch
the gulls begging for the catch. Then the cold soon
calls me home to warm by the fire. To sleep again. To
dream. To face my never-ending and terrible ordeal
all over again.

For weeks, I battled against my watery nightmare. I
refused to sleep. I'd sit up all through the night and
watch the ghostly fog roll in over the sea. I couldn't
eat. I became so exhausted that I didn't know if I was
awake or asleep anymore.

Finally, I decided to flee. To find a haven from this
haunting. In a desperate bid for escape.

As I say, I had lived in that place all my life. I am not from here. I came here only in the hope to make my getaway. To escape my dreams. But lately, I find myself waking with a start, covered in sweat.

Confused and dazed as before, I make my way outside to walk along the river in the early morning light. Then, as was my old habit, I carry myself back home to fall asleep again. To dream again! To sink! To drown! To remember!

"Oh, she has followed me here!
The Queen of the Sea!
Searching for me.
Sending her underwater world to surround me
To beckon me back to the sea."

FX: Sound effect-Sea sounds
FX: Lights fade to black
FX: Projections out for 'Queen of the Sea'
FX: Sound effect-Sea sounds fade out.

Phobic Couple, **PLAYERS #1, #2,** cross the bridge and make their way to the Central Platform.

FX: Lights/ Central Platform

PLAYER #2
Don't tell anyone, but I can't cut into melons, tomatoes, peppers, or marrows. It just makes my skin crawl. I have to drop the knife and leave the kitchen. It's the seeds, you see? Blimey! I can't even say the word.

PLAYER #1

I go rigid if I am in a room with a fish tank. And I couldn't possibly touch a fish to save my life.

I cannot watch fish on the internet or television either. Also, swimming is off the cards in case I come across a fish in the water. So, there you have it. I don't like fish.
(Exeunt)

SOLO PHOBIC PERFORMANCE #3

FX: Lights crossfade to 'Divertissement' area.
FX: Sound- 'The Itsy, Bitsy Spider' Nursery Rhyme
FX: Projection of assorted spiders

(Arachnophobia) a **PLAYER** sits on the floor with their hands over their eyes. They repeat the following in a stage whisper throughout.

PLAYER

"Spiders! They're coming to get me! Oh my! My heart's pounding! I feel dizzy! I can't breathe! Is that one touching me? I think I'm going to pass out. Ug!"

FX: Lights in Divertissement area fade to black.
FX: Projection out
FX: Sound fades out

PLAYERS #5, #6 in position on Central Platform for 'Phobophobia'

PHOBOPHOBIA

A **Doctor**, **PLAYER #5**, sits behind an empty desk.
There is a second chair facing the desk. **Julian**,
PLAYER #6, enters warily. He is dressed completely
in black and wears dark sunglasses.

JULIAN
(He looks over his shoulder as if he is being followed)
Hello. My name's Julian. I'm an actor.

DOCTOR
Hello, Julian. Please sit down.
(**Doctor** mimes answering a phone.)
"Not just now, Alice. I'm with a patient."
(He mimes replacing the receiver)
(To **Julian**) Pardon me.

JULIAN
(Very suspiciously) Why do you have a beard? I
don't like beards. Are you a hipster?

DOCTOR
I'm sorry if it upsets you.

JULIAN
It upsets me.

DOCTOR
Sorry

JULIAN
Forget it… I have a problem, Doctor. Actually, I have
a lot of problems.

DOCTOR
You can call me Bill.

JULIAN
I have a lot of problems, Bill.

DOCTOR
How may I help?

JULIAN
(Standing)
This chair sucks. This chair is shite.

DOCTOR
Make yourself comfortable.

JULIAN
And turn down the lights, why don't you? Are you
trying to blind me?

DOCTOR
(He mimes dimming the lights)

FX: Lights dimmed/Central Platform

DOCTOR
Better?

JULIAN
Somewhat, yes. I suppose so.

DOCTOR
You were saying?

JULIAN
I said, "I suppose so." I suppose so! Are you deaf?

DOCTOR
No, I meant to say tell me more about your problems.

JULIAN
Right. Sorry. I'm on edge. It's my nerves. They're shot.

DOCTOR
Relax, if you can. Take your time.

JULIAN
This could take a while. I have a lot of problems. I don't know where to start.

DOCTOR
Start at the start. Tell me about these problems.

JULIAN
Okay. (He breathes deeply) I was reading this book. I shouldn't have done! It has messed with my mind.

I can't think straight anymore. Since I read this book, everything bothers me now. Everything agitates me.

JULIAN
(Continuing)
I can't eat. I can't sleep. I can't stay in. I can't go out.
I'm afraid of everything! 'Panophobic'-that's what I
am.

DOCTOR
Panophobic?

JULIAN
Panophobia! Panophobia! You're a doctor, aren't
you, Bill? Don't you know what panophobia means?

DOCTOR
I believe I do.

JULIAN
Panophobia. Fear of everything. I am afraid of
everything!

DOCTOR
I know what it means.

JULIAN
Then why ask me?

DOCTOR
What makes you feel you are panophobic?

JULIAN
The book. It was the book that convinced me. I'm
researching a role for a play I'm doing.

JULIAN
(Continuing)
It's all about phobias. So, I'm reading this book and it explains everything about them. You know, fear of beards, fear of light, fear of smell… Crikey! It stinks in here!

DOCTOR
I didn't notice.

JULIAN
It smells of rotten fish.

DOCTOR
Does it?

JULIAN
I don't like fish.

DOCTOR
I see.

JULIAN
Open a window, won't you? But not too much! I don't like noise either. Or the wind. Or the rain. Or the cold or the heat or oh bloody hell!

DOCTOR
(Rising, he mines opening a window)
How's that?

JULIAN
(He takes a deep breath)
That's it! Perfect.

DOCTOR
(Returning to sit)
Good. So, tell me more about this book of yours. It
seems to have disturbed you a great deal.

JULIAN
Of course, it did. That's why I came to see you. This
book-this diabolical book- until I read this book, I
thought I was perfectly normal. Never dreamed that I
had a problem. I was afraid of nothing. Then, I read
this book. And do you know what?

DOCTOR
No. Tell me.

JULIAN
Now, I have a lot of problems, Bill. I have problems
on top of problems on top of problems.

DOCTOR
And you reckon this book is responsible for your
'problems'?

JULIAN
Too right. It goes on and on about every phobia
imaginable. I'm reading about wild things, Bill. Not
just garden variety fear of flying or heights or fire or
whatever, but wild, wild, things. There are people out
there who are afraid of chickens. Can you believe it?

There are poor souls who tremble at the sight of
worms. They faint at the thought of thunder. All kinds
of craziness. All kinds of things. People are phobic
about anything and everything. And now, now, I am
too.

DOCTOR
You fear such things yourself?

JULIAN
Yes. I have become infested with phobias.

DOCTOR
You feel you are infested?

JULIAN
Like a dog full of fleas.

DOCTOR
But you never experienced any of these fears prior to
the reading of this book?

JULIAN
Got it in one, Bill.

DOCTOR
You believe somehow that you have contracted these
phobias?

JULIAN
Every time I read about one of these phobias, I said to
myself, "I can see that" and blast! - if I didn't start
having the same fears myself. Now I am so
frightened of poultry, I can't even look at a chicken
sandwich!

DOCTOR
Yes, I can see how this might be a problem for you.

JULIAN
Good! But can you help me? I have a performance to
do. People are counting on me.

DOCTOR
I believe I can offer you help.

JULIAN
Then do it! I can't go on like this. I can't go on.

DOCTOR
There is no need for panic. I believe you may be
suffering from a delusion. In my opinion, your self-
diagnosis of panophobia is erroneous.

I do not believe, from what you have said, that you
are panophobic at all. You mentioned yourself that
you were afraid of nothing until you read this book of
yours.

JULIAN
That's true.

DOCTOR
What I believe has happened is that your research for
your role has triggered a classic case of
'Phobophobia'.

JULIAN
Phobophobia?

DOCTOR
That's right. Phobophobia. You are afraid of being
afraid.

JULIAN
Huh! I have phobophobia.

DOCTOR
Yes, that is my thinking. And I believe that your condition will disappear once you leave this performance behind you.

JULIAN
It's only temporary?

DOCTOR
I believe so. You said yourself that you read about 'wild' fears and could identify with them. As a result, you became afraid that you might have these fears too. Try not to worry. Your phobic infestation, as you call it, will fade away at the final curtain call.

JULIAN
It will go away as easily as that?

DOCTOR
Very likely. If not, come back and see me.

JULIAN
Thank you, Bill.

DOCTOR
I hope that I have been of some help. When does your show open?

JULIAN
Tonight

FX: Lights/Blackout
FX: Projections out for 'Phobophobia'

Performance Art Section 4

FX: PA music as necessary for Live Music #4 set-up.
FX: PA music out/ lights up in 'Divertissement' area.
Live Music #4

FX: At end of live music set, lights out in
'Divertissement' area

FX: Projection for 'Phobic Dance #3'.

Dancers in position for entrance to Central Platform
for 'Phobic Dance #3'

FX: Projections up for 'Phobic Dance #3'
FX: Lights/Central Platform for 'Phobic Dance #3
FX: Sound effect-bats flying
FX: Sound effect segues to 'Bat Music' selection.

PHOBIC DANCE #3-Chiroptophobia

*A dance piece choreographed to express a fear of
bats, Chiroptophobia.
In the original production, the dancers were
costumed as bats and entered en masse across the
bridge while accompanied by the sound of bats flying.
An acrobatic dance commenced on the Central
Platform as the sound effect segued into the selected
dance music.*

At conclusion of 'Phobic Dance #3'…

FX: Lights/music out
FX: 'Phobic Dance #3' projections out

FX*:* Projections up for 'Balloon Lady'
FX: Sound effect-In the dark, we hear the sound of balloons popping and being pulled and stretched.

PLAYER #3 in position on Central Platform

FX: Lights/Central Platform

BALLOON LADY

FX: Sound effect of balloons popping gradually peters out.

A woman costumed in a balloon-like outfit, directly addresses the audience.

PLAYER #3
I don't like balloons. Balloons terrify me. If I never saw another balloon again, it would still be too soon. I do not like balloons. I do not like them. Period. Good. Now you know. I don't want to see, touch, or hear about balloons.

I dread when they're popped or hear that awful squeaky, skin-crawling noise when they are scraped along their surface. I tremble if they are hung overhead.

They have made my life a misery. They have made me look ridiculous. They have actually caused me injury.

So, please. No balloon jokes. No creeping up behind me with a balloon to tease me. You may think it's funny, but it is nothing short of sadism pure and simple. Balloons for me are not festive and fun. They are positively revolting. There. I couldn't possibly be any clearer than that.

I was perfectly normal about balloons until I was a teenager. Then one day, we were having a birthday bash for my younger twin sisters. You know, cake, ice cream, games, and of course balloons.

Uncle Teddy was there-he was still around in those days- and he thought of himself as the 'life of the party'. I was standing in the background posing and pretending. I was far too sophisticated for such nonsense.
(You see? Just a normal, typical teenager.)

But then Uncle Ted picked up a balloon and began squeezing it like he was going to make it burst. This set the children off and they started squealing and running about with their fingers in their ears.

For some reason, the sight of this affected me quite strongly. I ran into the loo, locked the door, and put my fingers in my ears too, so I would not hear that balloon pop.

I emerged a minute or so later, appearing impeccably cool, but something snapped in me that day and ever since, balloons have always horrified me.

How I wish this could be sorted! I know it's ridiculous, but now if I am in a room with an inflated balloon, I go all funny inside. I feel sick and giddy and if I don't leave at once, I faint.

Usually, I can avoid 'Balloon Situations', as my husband calls them, but parties can be an absolute nightmare. We have two small children ourselves and, of course, they go to parties with the other kids and play with balloons.

I always stand at the door, pretending that I am 'in a rush', when I come to collect them. I wouldn't dare face going inside.

I'm depriving my kids of having birthday parties of their own. I am in terror that little Simon or Allison or whoever will show up with a bag of balloons. And I would be exposed as the terrific ninny that I am.

I know this is awful to say, but I hate Christmas. New Year's Eve celebrations too. They are the only times when 'Balloon Situations' just can't be avoided. You never know when I balloon might appear.

I ask my husband to scour the room to look for any balloons lurking there. And I refuse to take a step inside until he returns and gives me the all-clear.

Last year, one of the guests at our Christmas party found out about my little secret and chased me around the house with a balloon. As I say, some people just will not accept that I am petrified of them.

I burst into tears and ran and locked myself in our bathroom for over an hour. I sat there in the tub crying and shaking all over. I ignored the knocks at the door. I covered my ears not to hear the voices calling out to me from outside. I felt absolutely humiliated. I really would rather have jumped from a cliff than have that balloon near me.

And New Year's Eve is even worse. Once, I actually knocked myself unconscious at a New Year's Eve do. At the stroke of midnight, balloons began floating down from above and I went into full-blown hysterics.

The club was packed and I flung myself about desperate for escape, tripped, and banged my head on the floor-hard. I was out like a light.

If you knew how I felt, you wouldn't laugh. I always need to be on guard. I avoid social occasions, when I think balloons may be involved. It's crippling, sickening, and totally embarrassing.

Oh! The sight of them, the thought of touching them, makes my skin crawl. And the noise of them being burst or 'pulled around' with that hellish squeak is just unbearable.

Sometimes, when children find out about another child's fear, they can be quite cruel. But when adults find out about my peculiar balloon 'issue', they can be every bit as bad.

"You're not really afraid of balloons, are you?", they say with a laugh. "Come on! Look at this one! It won't hurt you! Just touch it." Or worse are the sadists with their 'Here comes Balloon Man' jokes. Ha, ha, bloody ha. Because you see, it's really not a laughing matter at all.

OTHER PLAYERS
(Off-stage)
♫ "For she's a jolly good fellow
For she's a jolly good fellow
For she's a jolly good fellow
And so say all of us!" ♫

Off-stage, **PLAYERS** burst balloons. Laughter. **PLAYER #3** looks around in panic. She paces frantically on the Central Platform, but cannot decide from where the sounds are coming. She covers her ears.

FX: Lights/Central Platform fade to black
FX: Projections out for 'Balloon Lady'

Phobic Couple, **PLAYERS #1, #2,** cross the bridge and make their way to the Central Platform.

FX: Lights/Central Platform

PLAYER #1
I can't believe that I'm the only one who is terrified of this.

PLAYER #1
(Continuing)
Don't you hate it when people trim their nails right in front of you? It makes me go all hot and clammy. And my tummy starts churning and I feel really ill. I don't know. Maybe it's just me.

PLAYER #2
In her biography of Sir Richard Burton, his wife Sally said that he could not sit in a room, if he knew a jar of honey was there. Even if it was hidden in a drawer or cupboard. Weird.

PLAYER #1
I am afraid of fire. Deathly afraid. If I am asked to visit someone at a building where I've never been before, I always ask them to send me the fire escape plans first. That way I can plan ahead.
(Exeunt)

FX: Lights out/Central Platform

FX: Projections up for 'Phobic Dance #4

Dancers in position on Central Platform
Jugglers in position in Divertissement and Bridge areas

FX: Lights/Central Platform and Music for 'Phobic Dance #4.
FX: Lights/Divertissement and Bridge area on cue from dance music.

PHOBIC DANCE #4-Pyrophobia

A dance piece choreographed to express a fear of fire, Pyrophobia.

In the original production, a combination of dancers and jugglers, who simulated juggling fire, filled the Central Platform, Bridge, and Divertissement areas. A 'Fire Dance' began on the Central Platform and on a cue in the selected dance music, lights illuminated the jugglers on the Bridge and Divertissement areas.

At conclusion of 'Phobic Dance #4'…
FX: Lights/music out
FX: 'Phobic Dance #4' projections out

FX*: Projections up for 'Lifts'

PLAYERS #1, #6 in position on Central Platform for 'Lifts'

FX: Lights/Central Platform

LIFTS

In silence, **PLAYERS #1, #6**, stand side by side.
PLAYER #6 looks up and then looks around at his surroundings occasionally.
He is struggling to remain calm and relaxed. He begins whistling nervously for a moment and then hums to himself. He grows more and more anxious, looks around furtively, and listens for noises.
PLAYER #6 then breathes deeply and noisily in another attempt to calm himself.

PLAYER #1 remains perfectly calm and still throughout, except when cued by **PLAYER #6** for a reaction.

PLAYER #6
(Addressing the audience)

This is a lift simulation. This is not a real lift. This is a practice lift that goes neither up nor down. I'm practicing (Then indicating **PLAYER #1**), WE are practicing (**PLAYER #1** nods with a smile) being in a real lift together.

You see, about ten years ago now, I was leaving my office and made my way to the lift. A real lift. A working, functional lift. We were on the twelfth floor. I had been in this lift thousands of times before. I knew this lift. I had no problem with this lift and, as far as I knew, this lift had no problem with me.

Anyway, I get on the lift. It is full of other people. It's the end of the working day. Everyone wants to leave. We began our descent to the ground floor, when suddenly we hear a terrible grinding noise. You know, like a learner car driver grinding the gears.

The lift started to shudder and shake and with a jolt it stopped dead-still midstream. We were left literally hanging there in space. In silence.

At first, no one said anything. A couple of young office girls started giggling a bit. But everyone remained calm. The bloke near the lift control panel kept pressing and re-pressing the lobby button to no effect. We were just hanging there going nowhere.

56

No one could get a signal or their phones to call for help and this bloke would not stop pressing the lobby button. He kept jamming his thumb in there and growing more and more agitated every time he did it. "Bloody hell!" I heard him swear.

Then, this chap starts pressing the alarm button. A ringing sound filled the lift every time he pressed it. I think that's when it hit me. My lips felt dry. I started licking them. I was feeling hot and uncomfortable. I loosened my tie.

And there's the alarm bell ringing again! Everyone starts talking at the same time. I can't understand a word they're saying! The alarm! Ring! Ring! Ring! Then the smell! I could smell fear. It smells like fear.

I want to run, but there's no place to go. What's happening to me? My ears are drumming. My skin is oozing cold sweat. I feel faint.
Ring! Ring! Ring!

I hear a buzzing noise from inside my head. Everything starts looking warped, weird. Out of focus. I look around at the others and their faces look distorted like in a funhouse mirror.

Then everyone starts staring at me. Why are they staring at me?! I want to shout, but I can't speak.

My throat's so tight. I can't breathe! Things started spinning around me. Then blackness. Like I'm being swallowed up in a hole…Black.

The next thing I know, I'm in an ambulance. Medical
staff are all around me.

"Where am I?" "Who are you?" How'd I get here?"
There's an oxygen mask on my face.
"Breathe in and out slowly" someone tells me.
"Try to relax."

Someone pats me on the head to comfort me. "You
fainted in the lift," they say. Later, I learned it took
over an hour for us to be rescued.

Ever since then, I've always avoided lifts. Whenever I
see one, I am transported back to that day. I feel the
same feelings of being trapped and out of control. I
relive my embarrassment of fainting dead away. I
don't want to lose control. I don't want to feel
embarrassed again. That's what my therapist tells me.
When I feel trapped, she says, I try to sit on my
hysteria. But something has to give and if my mind
won't, then my body will. So I faint.

At the time, it seemed to me that I kept remarkable
self-control. Despite how I was feeling. Later, I heard
I blacked out within the first five minutes. Just
thinking of a packed lift, stuck between floors, and
me out cold, makes me feel nauseous. That can't
happen ever again. Never.

So, I avoid lifts. I walk up the twelve flights of stairs
to my office. And down again. Even at lunch.
It may take me five minutes to catch my breath
afterward, but I'd rather resign my position than take
the lift.

I also avoid taking the underground train now. I won't take the Tube in case it gets stuck in a tunnel. I now always leave my office door open too, so I won't feel trapped. Yes, it is getting worse.

Like the others trapped with me that day, I should have forgotten that incident on the lift by now. But it still haunts me. Common sense tells me that it's not likely to happen again. But, as my therapist says, my phobia has little to do with common sense.

So, now I'm taking 'The Treatment', as they call it. It has not been easy on me. For the first two weeks, I was told to try sitting in a cupboard under my stairs at home. At first, I had to keep the door open. I made my partner stand outside. But now, I can stay in that cupboard without anyone in the house. And the door shut. I am being 'acclimatized' my therapist promises me. So far, so good.

And here we are. We've 'graduated' to the lift simulation.

(To **PLAYER #1**)
It's not too bad, is it?

(**PLAYER #1** smiles and nods in agreement)

PLAYER #6
(To audience)
Of course, there is no door. No buttons. No mechanism. But it's a step.
(To **PLAYER #1**)
We're not going to tell ourselves that we have no control over this lift, are we?

(**PLAYER #1** firmly shakes his head 'no')

PLAYER #6
(To audience)
We won't think it could plummet to the ground once
we get in. Or it might get stuck again. I'm breathing
calmly. Control my breath. There's plenty of air. I
won't think there's no air.

(Starting to pant, he turns to **PLAYER #1**)
PLAYER #6
(Continuing)
It seems to me the lack of air… no air…no air…

(**PLAYER #1** suddenly collapses heavily to the floor)

PLAYER #6
(Staring down at the prone **PLAYER #1** at his feet)
The lack of air… there's no air…

(**PLAYER #6** begins taking very deep breaths. He
removes a handkerchief from his pocket to wipe away
his perspiration. He starts whistling to distract himself
from and ignore the unconscious **PLAYER #1**)

PLAYER #6
(To audience)
Isn't it hot? You must feel it surely. It's so hot. It's
suffocating! Why don't they turn down the heat?
Or… Open a window! There's no air in here! Open a
window! Open a window! Let me out! I can't breathe.
There's no air. There's no air. There's…no…air!

FX: Lights/blackout
FX: Projections out for 'Lifts'

Performance Art Section 5

FX: PA music as required to cover set up for 'Hyperphobia Extravaganza'

As all **Players** move to position…
FX: PA music out.
FX: Projections up for 'Hyperphobia Extravaganza'
Projections change repeatedly throughout on cue.

HYPERPHOBIA EXTRAVAGANZA

FX: Lights/Bridge and Divertissement area

PLAYER #5 is alone on Bridge

PLAYERS #1, #2, #3, #4, #6, #7 are in a spatial configuration in the Divertissement area. They break from and back into this and other configurations on verbal cues from **PLAYER #5**.

PLAYER #5
Keraunophobia

PLAYER #7
Fear of thunder

PLAYER #5
Ichthyophobia

PLAYER #6
Fear of fish

PLAYER #5
Genuphobia

PLAYER #4
Fear of knees

PLAYER #5
Chrometophobia

PLAYER #3
Fear of money

PLAYER #5
Thalassophobia

PLAYER #2
Fear of the sea

PLAYER #5
Chionophobia

PLAYER #1
Fear of snow

FX: Projections change

All **PLAYERS** in Divertissement area move to a new spatial configuration as **PLAYER #5** continues.

DANCERS enter and move to position on Central Platform.

FX: Projections for 'Hyperphobia Dance'
FX: Lights/Central Platform
FX: Music for 'Hyperphobia Dance'

In the original production, this dance continued throughout the litany of named phobias to follow. The dancers combined and reprised sections of their earlier dances. Projections changed to images formerly seen as the dancers revisited motifs from earlier dances.

FX: PLAYER #5 now speaks through microphone

PLAYER #5
Ombrophobia

PLAYERS #6, #7
Fear of rain

PLAYER #5
Toxiphobia

PLAYERS #3, #4
Fear of poison

PLAYER #5
Siderophobia

PLAYERS #1, #2
Fear of stars

PLAYER #5
Odontophobia

PLAYERS #1, #2
Fear of teeth

PLAYER #5
Olfactophobia

PLAYERS #3, #4
Fear of smell

PLAYER #5
Algophobia

PLAYERS #6, #7
Fear of pain

All **PLAYERS** in Divertissement area move to a new spatial configuration. **PLAYER #5** increases tempo.

PLAYER #5
Hedonophobia

PLAYERS #4, #6, #7
Fear of pleasure

PLAYER #5
Iophobia

PLAYERS #1, #2, #3
Fear of rust

PLAYER #5
Sciophobia

PLAYERS #4, #6, #7
Fear of shadows

PLAYER #5
Potamophobia

PLAYERS #1, #2, #3
Fear of rivers

PLAYER #5
Phonophobia

PLAYERS #4, #6, #7
Fear of noise

PLAYER #5
Pyrophobia

PLAYERS #1, #2, #3
Fear of fire

FX: Projections change

All **PLAYERS** in Divertissement area move to a new spatial configuration as **PLAYER #5** continues.

PLAYER #5
(At an ever increasing tempo)
Pogonophobia

PLAYERS #1, #6
Fear of beards

PLAYER #5
Alektorophobia

PLAYERS #4, #7
Fear of chickens

PLAYER #5
Frigophobia

PLAYERS #1, #6
Fear of cold

PLAYER #5
Theophobia

PLAYERS #2, #3, #4, #7
Fear of God

PLAYER #5
Amathophobia

PLAYERS #1, #6
Fear of dust

PLAYER #5
Anglophobia

PLAYERS #1, #2, #3, #4, #6, #7
Fear of the English

FX: Light change

PLAYERS leave Divertissement area and march as a group through the audience area

PLAYER #5 increases tempo

PLAYER #5
Germanophobia

PLAYER #7
Fear of Germans

PLAYER #5
Kakorraphiaphobia

PLAYERS #6, #7
Fear of failure

PLAYER #5
Doraphobia

PLAYERS #4, #6, #7
Fear of fur

PLAYER #5
Chaetophobia

PLAYERS #3, #4, #6, #7
Fear of hair

PLAYER #5
Astrapophobia

PLAYERS #2, #3, #4, #6, #7
Fear of lightning

PLAYER #5
Androphobia

PLAYERS #1, #2, #3, #4, #6, #7
Fear of men

FX: Light change
PLAYERS leave audience area and form a new spatial configuration in the Divertissement area.

PLAYER #5 continues ever more quickly.

PLAYER #5
Gynophobia

PLAYERS #1, #2, #3, #4, #6, #7
Fear of women

PLAYER #5
Chromatophobia

PLAYERS #2, #3, #4, #6, #7
Fear of colours

PLAYER #5
Barophobia

PLAYERS #3, #4, #6, #7
Fear of gravity

PLAYER #5
Hippophobia

PLAYERS #4, #6, #7
Fear of horses

PLAYER #5
Dikephobia

PLAYERS #6, #7
Fear of justice

PLAYER #5
Photophobia

PLAYER #7
Fear of light

PLAYERS in Divertissement area now form a tableau which quickly changes shape as each subsequent phobia is announced by **PLAYER #5**.

FX: Lights pulse and strobe in Divertissement area along with the changing tableau

PLAYER #5
Nyctophobia

PLAYERS #1, #2, #3, #4, #6, #7
Fear of darkness

PLAYER #5
Helminthophobia

PLAYERS #1, #2, #3, #4, #6, #7
Fear of worms

PLAYER #5
Dendrophobia

PLAYERS #1, #2, #3, #4, #6, #7
Fear of trees

PLAYER #5
Scabiophobia

PLAYERS #1, #2, #3, #4, #6, #7
Fear of itching

PLAYER #5
Linonophobia

PLAYERS #1, #2, #3, #4, #6, #7
Fear of string

PLAYER #5
Panophobia

PLAYERS #1, #2, #3, #4, #6, #7
Fear of everything!!!

All **PLAYERS** and **DANCERS** freeze

FX: Lights blackout
FX: 'Hyperphobia Dance' Music out
FX: Projections out

All **PLAYERS** and **DANCERS** exit in blackout

PLAYER #5 makes quick costume change back to
DOCTOR character and then crosses to the Central
Platform
FX: Lights/Central Platform

PLAYER #5
(Addressing the audience)
If you are feeling in any way phobic as a result of
tonight's performance…

(**PLAYER #4** screams from off-stage)

PLAYER #5
There is no need for panic.

(PLAYERS #2, #3, #4 scream off stage)

PLAYER #5
I believe your anxiety will dissipate once you leave
this performance behind.

(PLAYERS #1, #6, #7 scream off stage)

PLAYER #5
I recommend some soothing chamomile tea, a hot
bath (no bubbles), and a good night's sleep.
Good night!
(Exit)

FX: Lights-Blackout
FX: PA music for Bows
FX: Lights for Bows.

-END-

DREAMLAND

Charles Serio

ORIGINAL CAST AND CREDITS

Written and directed: Charles Serio
Design: Mari Cardew-Richardson, assisted by
Camilla Bak Oleson
Choreography: Karin Trembeth
Lighting: Peter Wright
Costumier: Lisa Kyriacou
Make-up: Debbie Parker
PA Music: Christophe Lambert and 4 Tel

PLAYERS:

Jerome Blake
Michele Brach
Jean Buckland
Ella Hofmann
Deborah Hood
Deanna Johnson
Karen Lennon
Allan Lochhead
Meri Pakarinen
Karin Trembeth
Julian Shaw
William Simpson
Ruth Werner

CONTRIBUTING ARTISTS:

John Pettenuzzo, Lulu Martin, Christian Velasquez,
Neil Hague, Rob Selkirk, Dan Parker,
Amanda/Robert Sym and other local artists

MUSICIANS:

Graeme Selkirk, Korus, Beat Route, Iroquim, and Hildegard Maier

Dreamland premiered in London at The Pigeon Loft Theatre, October 1997.

Dreamland is a mixed performance arts piece divided into two distinct and separated areas- a Club area and a Performance area. It combines elements of theatre, live music, dance, visual arts, and media arts.

The **Dreamland** performance repeats itself on a recurring basis. In the Club area, live music sets of roughly twenty to thirty minutes are performed throughout the evening.

As each music set concludes, a cue from the PA system signals that the next **Dreamland** performance will begin.

FX: PA music cue
FX: Lights/Performance area

Two characters, costumed and made-up as 'Sandmen', **PLAYERS #1, #2**, enter the Club area and choose a selection of the audience to enter the performance half of the venue.

The Sandmen serve as custodians to lead the audience through the performance area and keep them together as one group. The audience selected is led through an archway entrance to the Dreamland area. After the selected audience passes through the archway entrance, PA music continues in the Club area. When the Dreamland performance is completed, the selected audience is led back to the Club area by the two 'Sandmen'. Another selection of the audience is then chosen and led into the Dreamland enclosure.

The Dreamland performance is repeated in a loop.

SET

In the original production, a large, dividing, sound-proofed screen/curtain was erected to separate the Club area from the Performance enclosure.

There is an archway entrance through this dividing curtain where the Sandmen, **PLAYERS #1, #2**, lead the selected audience.

The archway leads into a long, red-lit entrance corridor. This area contains visual artwork, sound effects, and sculpture with a dream-like theme.

FX: Dream music
FX: Silhouette Light

As the audience views the artwork, a silhouette of a **PLAYER** is projected. The silhouetted figure sings the lyrics of a dream-based song a cappella.

At the far end of the red-lit corridor, **ZOLTAR**, a fantastical fairy princess on roller blades, waits in stillness. She stands at another hidden entrance to the main performance area.

At the conclusion of the dream-based song, the Sandmen, **PLAYERS #1, #2**, lead the audience toward **ZOLTAR** who then skates away from the red-lit corridor leading the audience into the remaining performance areas.

FX: Lights change
FX: PA Music change for **'Daydream'** Section

The main performance area is divided into **four** sections inside a large white fabric rectangle. The audience is led by the Sandmen, **PLAYERS #1, #2**, into a **'Daydream'** section (Section1) which consists of sculptural pieces and other oddities based on dream themes.

FX: Light change
FX: PA music change for **'Nightmare Visions'** Section

The audience is then led into a **'Nightmare Visions'** section (Section 2) of a more harrowing nature. This area features multi-media presentations, music, and sound effects appropriate to this theme.

At the conclusion of the 'Nightmare Visions' section, The Sandmen, **PLAYERS #1, #2**, lead the audience as one group into a large **Open Performance** area (Section 3).

FX: Light change
FX: PA music change for **'Open Performance'** area

As the audience enters, six **PLAYERS** are frozen in a sleeping pose. As the performance begins, these **PLAYERS** come to life on a cue from **ZOLTAR**.

ZOLTAR skates to a central position among the six sleeping **PLAYERS**. **PLAYERS #3, #4, #5** to her right and **PLAYERS #6, #7, #8** to her left.

The Sandmen, **PLAYERS #1, #2**, stand at either end of the audience to define the playing area and separating the **PLAYERS** from the audience itself.

FX: Lights change

ZOLTAR
I am Zoltar
From a far off star
Seller of dreams.

I am Zoltar
From a far off star
Dealer in destiny.

A butterfly (**PLAYER #7** rises)
A woman in black (**PLAYER #5** rises)
A spinning wheel (**PLAYER #3** rises)
A still pool of water (**PLAYER #4** rises)
Listening to whispers (**PLAYER #8** rises)
Images of days past (**PLAYER #6** rises)

All the things that live in dreams
Are Zoltar's to command.

PLAYER #3

(In a steady, flowing, mellifluous cadence. As if
inducing a hypnotic trance in the audience.)

Good evening. Welcome to **Dreamland.** Now before
we begin, it is essential for us all to relax. Let me help
you get into a dream-like state. Start by breathing
deeply. In and out. Go ahead. Breathe along with my
cadence in speaking.

That's right. In and out. And while you breathe along
with my words, reach out and take your neighbour's
hand. Go on. And breathe together as one…. Breathe
in… and… Breathe out. Together and as one.
In…and out…good…fine…Keep breathing as one.
Together.

Now while you have been led through the archway
that brought you here, there is still another archway to
pass through…in your mind… through which you
must pass. For the land of dreams does not exist in
space or time, but exists beyond them both…. And
the key to that dream door… the door to your
dreams…is already in your possession…dwelling
inside us all.

FX: Light change

Let me help you… to help yourself…to find this entry
key…to **Dreamland**…that we all possess…

PLAYER #3
(Continuing)
Let me ask you to do something…if you will…while
you breathe together…simply close your eyes...if you
may…while you breathe together…or leave them
open…if you prefer…

And as you sit comfortably
together…breathing…create in your mind's eye a
clear, rich…focused, visual image… of a wall. Can
you see it? Let yourself see it.

And on that wall you will see three doors. Let
yourself see them. Side-by-side…. And you
realise…as you see these doors…that the one farthest
to your right…
will lead you to someplace… familiar…

And as you continue looking…at these doors...you
can sense… that the one…farthest to your left…will
lead you somewhere that at first appears…
unusual…but once inside…you will discover you
have already been there before…

FX: Lights change

Now, there is another door, is there not?...feel
yourself walking up to that third door…the one in the
middle…and put your hand up against it…

But as you push, **you will not be able to open that
door yourself**…it may open in a way…that you have
never had a door…open before…go ahead…and try
in vain to push it open…it is hopeless to try…

PLAYER #3
(Continuing)

Search this door instead…until you find some special characteristic…special to you…which has meaning for you…to allow you to open this door…in a way that a door has never opened before…

FX: Lights change

PLAYER #3
(Continuing)

Now very slowly… I want you to prepare yourself to step through the threshold of this door…but before you step through…I want you to realise…that you are walking into a new experience…something you will never have experienced before… there will be elements and images there…that will make no sense whatsoever…and you will have no words for these elements…

And yet they will become the most important things of all…to you personally…to what is inside you…as a person…in ways you do not fully understand… and as you notice these elements…as they become more and more significant to you…pay close attention…there is a meaning there for you…something that will delight you…surprise you…amaze you…

FX: Light change

PLAYER #3
(Continuing)

Now! **Walk through this door!**… Stride boldly over the threshold…and when you turn around… you will see there is no door anymore.

Look around your new environment…look for what is personally significant to you…Look with clarity… look with depth...

Because there is something there…that you have not noticed yet…let your mind's eye scan up and down and around…around this new, undiscovered world…for you will not know what is significant to you until you pass it…then it will fall into place… That's right… then you will know… then you will see…when you turn back and look again…nothing will ever be quite the same again…for you have found what you always were looking for without knowing that you were looking for it…

And as you turn and head back… the door suddenly reappears right before your mind's eye…and as you cross the threshold again and return here…use it as your opportunity…as a reminder…of something you needed to know for quite some time…

And allow yourself… to draw from this experience…to renew yourself… to refresh yourself… and return to me here…in your own time…at your own rate…rejoin me here in this space…to begin your experience of **Dreamland.**

FX: PA music out
FX: Lights change for 'Psychic Calls #1'

9

PSYCHIC CALLS #1

PLAYERS #6, #7 address the audience in turn.

PLAYER #7

Spiritual answers from authentic psychics. Dreams interpreted. Don't delay! Text us now! Credit card payments happily accepted.

PLAYER #6

I am Mother Love. Contact me on my authentic love hotline. Is love in your future? Mother Love knows. Don't miss your one chance for happiness.

PLAYER #7

Free your soul! Open your mind. See your destiny through the 3rd eye. Miracles do happen, but first you must ask. Contact me, Zelda, the world's most powerful psychic! Click my banner now!

PLAYER #6

Let our professional psychics reveal the unknown in your future. Subscribe now for personal online psychic updates that will transform your life. Contact us now, now, now!

FX: Lights change for 'Coma Dreamers'

COMA DREAMERS

PLAYER #8

Dreamline: Cambridge. 'Coma Victims Waking up all over the World and Baffled Doctors don't know Why!'

The Department of Clinical Neurosciences at Cambridge University published a study today revealing that doctors worldwide are bewildered by reports of a bizarre, global phenomenon. Coma victims appear to be spontaneously awakening with all their mental faculties intact.
Over the past few weeks, more than seven hundred patients across the globe, many of whom had been brain dead and on life-support for over a year, have now mysteriously regained consciousness.

All of the patients reported a common experience.

One of the former coma victims who suddenly found herself awake stated…

PLAYER #4

"I felt like I was waking from a dream. I remember being in a brightly lit tunnel with lots of other people. We were all walking down this brightly lit tunnel. I don't know why. It just seemed to be the right thing to do."

PLAYER #8

Others claim to have been riding on a slowly-moving platform to a place with a bland, treeless landscape that was neither unpleasant nor enjoyable.

PLAYER #8
(Continuing)
The victims all say that they simply awoke, as if from a dream, after hearing a voice whispering in their ears, "It's time to go back".

PLAYER #4
"I felt as if I was travelling to somewhere. I didn't know where. I just stayed with the crowd. But when I heard that whispering voice telling me to go back, I just turned around and…Here I am!"

PLAYER #8
Medical specialists have been conducting psychological and neurological tests on the patients. They are hoping to create a profile which may explain a common factor behind this. But so far, these people appear to be very different from one another. All they seem to have in common is this experience. As noted German neurologist, Dr. Herta Stengel said…

PLAYER #3
"The amazing thing is that they all now have normal brain function. This has completely puzzled us and there appears to be no rational explanation."

PLAYER #8
Lucy Fellows-Smote, 43, is one of the lucky ones. She had been officially declared 'brain dead'. But she awoke a few weeks ago after more than fourteen months on life-support following an automobile accident.

PLAYER #5

"The place I went to was colourless and sandy. Like a monochrome desert without heat. There were others wandering around there, but none of us spoke to one another."

"I had the impression that we had been sent there to think, without distraction, about our lives and our world."

"The voice that ordered us to return didn't tell us why it was sending us back. Only that it was important for us to come back here."

PLAYER #8

Dr. Stengel, 53, refused to speculate on the reasons behind these baffling incidents.

PLAYER #3

"At present, we are keeping an open mind subject to further study. We are unsure, at the moment, why this has been happening. We do not know all that occurs in the brains of coma victims. They may well be experiencing what we refer to as 'coma dreaming'. What they report may be the result of these dreams and not based in reality. However, the fact that patients, previously classified as brain dead, also reported these same visions is highly curious indeed."

FX: Lights change for 'Psychic Calls #2'

PSYCHIC CALLS #2

PLAYERS #4, #6 address the audience in turn.

PLAYER #4

Let the ancient spirits guide you toward love and happiness. Contact us now for a genuine Native American dream reading! Results guaranteed.

PLAYER #6

Lonely? Discouraged? Confused? Find your soul mate. Gain wealth. Reverse evil influences. The answers are in your stars. Contact us today for a free initial consultation.

PLAYER #4

Contact us now at the 'Psychics of Salem' network. Our Wiccan psychics are caring, gifted, and in touch with the world of dreams. Let them interpret where your dreams are leading you.

PLAYER #6

Locally-sourced Aboriginal Dream-catchers for sale. Get them while supplies last. Absolutely genuine and accurate. Capture your dreams. Find the love and the fortune your dream life reveals. Money back guaranteed, if you are not fully satisfied. Order now!

FX: Lights change for 'Tabloid Nightmare'

TABLOID NIGHTMARE

PLAYER #5

Dreamline: Buenos Aires. 'Housewife Fried when Hairdryer Overheats!'

14

PLAYER #5
(Continuing)
A housewife having her hair permed at an Argentine beauty salon tragically died on Wednesday when her hairdryer overheated and caught fire.

Local police claimed, when they arrived at the salon, that the woman's head had been baked to a crisp.

Mother of two, Eva Ortega, was pronounced dead at the scene of the mishap at the Casa Manana Beauty Bar.

Authorities stated that the hairdryer must have exceeded temperatures of 250 degrees Celsius before stunned salon workers discovered the malfunction.

A police officer who witnessed the grisly scene said,

PLAYER #7
"The dryer must have overheated very quickly and Mrs. Ortega passed out before she could signal for help. Her head was so hot, we had to wait for more than twenty minutes before we could touch it. Right now, we are trying to find out why the machine went haywire. We highly recommended that the salon owner not use that dryer again."

PLAYER #5
According to Buenos Aires police, Mrs. Ortega went to the beauty salon for what hairstylists call a 'curly perm'.

PLAYER #5
(Continuing)
The 34 year old woman was placed under the high-powered hairdryer and sat quietly reading a fashion magazine.

A towel-boy, known only as Little Pablo, said at one point he saw the woman twitching under the dryer.

SANDMAN #1
(As 'Little Pablo')
"But I thought she had simply fallen asleep and was dreaming."

PLAYER #5
But after half and hour, salon owner, Maria Anado Cortez, checked on the woman and discovered the awful truth.

PLAYER #6
"It's all such a tragedy. She would have looked wonderful in that perm. I told her at the start that it would take years off her. And now we'll never know."

PLAYER #5
Little Pablo claimed even the curlers had melted.

SANDMAN #1
(As 'Little Pablo')
"It's just a nightmare. I keep thinking that I'll wake up and find this awful business never happened."

SANDMAN #1
(As 'Little Pablo' Continuing)
"If only she had managed to call out, we could have rescued her. And I would not have lost my tip. It really was a Bad Hair Day."

FX: Lights change

ZOLTAR
(In Finnish or any language with which the audience would be largely unfamiliar)

I am Zoltar
From a far off star
Seller of dreams.

I am Zoltar
From a far off star
Dealer in destiny.

A darkened staircase
A piano tinkling
A mystery stranger
A siren screaming
Muffled voices in the distance
Seeing the stars.

All the things that live in dreams
Are Zoltar's to command.

FX: Light change for 'Dreams of Abduction'
FX: UFO sounds

DREAMS OF ABDUCTION

PLAYER #4

Dreamline: Scarborough. 'I ate Dinner- with Space Aliens!'

FX: UFO sounds fade out

Scarborough, England. Rattled caravan owner, Clive Cooper, claimed to have been whisked aboard a spaceship in the Yorkshire Dales and treated to a bizarre, six-course, 'alien' feast.

The fare included such extra terrestrial delicacies as green eels, lizard livers, and eyeball lasagna! As the flabbergasted estate agent recalled…

SANDMAN #2

(As 'Clive Cooper')
"Some of it was rather tasty. But most of it smelled and tasted awful. I could barely choke it down."

"And once they told me what I was eating, it just made matters worse. But they were so nice, and trying so hard to please me, that I ate everything I could and just kept smiling. I didn't wish to appear impolite, you see."

PLAYER #4

Clive's spine-chilling adventure unfolded on 16th July last year as the Scarborough native camped alone in an isolated section of the Yorkshire Dales National Park. As the 44 year old father of three explained…

SANDMAN #2
"I was building a fire at sunset and settling down for
the night, when I heard the oddest noise. A strange,
unearthly whirring sound came from directly above
me and when I looked up, I saw this thing-this
silvery, egg-shaped, gray spaceship about 40 feet
across-land on the river bank directly across from my
camp."

"I wanted to run, but I was so stunned I was frozen in
my tracks."

PLAYER #4
Terrified Clive watched in wonder as three pasty-
faced blue-gray figures with black-slit eyes and
enormous mouths emerged from the craft. He claimed
that they then approached him and- in perfect
English- invited him aboard their vessel for dinner.

SANDMAN #2
"I thought I must be dreaming. I kept blinking and
pinching myself to make myself wake up. But it was
no good. I was already wide awake. I don't care what
anyone says. I was awake!"

PLAYER #4
Clive claims the aliens told him they were serving the
finest cuisine their planet had to offer.

SANDMAN #2
"And I couldn't pass up an offer like that."

PLAYER #4

Once aboard the mysterious craft, the nervous Earthling stated that he was joined by eight other aliens for a colossal feast which included:

- Juicy, green eels that tasted of seaweed and vinegar and had the consistency of slugs.

- Crispy intestines which the ET's said came from a six-foot long lizard-like creature that roams their native habitat.

- And a lasagna-like concoction, which the aliens informed Clive, included the pulverized eyeballs of a featherless bird called a 'Darrow'.

SANDMAN #2

"I think my favourite was something they called a 'Brokka'. I was instructed to eat everything-fur, feet, eyes, guts, brains-everything, and mighty tasty it was too. I know it sounds dreadful. But I scarfed the lot. Delicious!"

PLAYER #4

After the three-hour feast was finished, the aliens and their guest downed a syrupy white liquid called 'Hoosh' which Clive described as...

SANDMAN #2

"Potent stuff that smelled of ammonia and rotten eggs. After a few rounds of that brew, my hosts started to giggle in unison and we all ended up in a group hug. It was nice!"

PLAYER #4
And with that, the aliens escorted their well-fed guest
off their spaceship and soon quickly zoomed away to
the heavens.

A perplexed Clive added…

SANDMAN #2
"I don't know why they chose me to be their dinner
companion. But I hope they come back."

"That 'Brokka' was better than anything I ever ate in
my life. It tasted a little like chicken. It was truly
dreamy, but no matter what anyone says, I wasn't
dreaming!"

FX: Lights change for 'Dream Poem'

DREAM POEM

PLAYER #8
It's a déjà vu
It happened to you
It's a dream, a lie

It's a lullabye
It's a dream.

We're dreaming
We've drifted away
We're in another galaxy.

There's a road
There's a wall
There's a waterfall

PLAYER #8
(Continuing)
There are clouds floating in your mind
There's a bump in the night
A case of stage fright

There's a mysterious man you think you know
Now he's a woman in red
Near a flower bed
Dancing in dumb show.

A quick jump to the stairs
Now you're tumbling there
Down, down, tumbling down
You're a camera following in slo-mo.

You're atop a hill
You're near a windmill
You hear voices whispering inside
That someone has died
Or was it they lied
That the Queen of Hearts has gone?

A tunnel
A chase
A frightened embrace
Bouquets abandoned on the roadside.

It's a déjà vu
It happened to you
It's a dream, a lie
It's a lullabye
It's a dream.

FX: Lights change for 'L'Oolaloo'

22

L'OOLALOO

PLAYER #6

Dreamline: Paris. 'We were looking for Atlantis in the Wrong Ocean!'

Paris, France- Atlantis, the mythical undersea empire, may lie beneath the depths of the Pacific.

The underwater kingdom might still be thriving today on the floor of the Pacific Ocean, a French archeologist reports.

The world-renowned archeologist, Dr. Diana Brulet, often referred to as the French 'In-Diana Jones', claimed that ancient maps unearthed at an undisclosed archeological dig last November place the fabled lost continent about 2,500 miles west of Peru.

Documents uncovered at the site suggest that highly evolved human-like creatures were the original inhabitants of Atlantis. And that later they adapted their cities to survive undersea life just before the empire sank without a trace.

As Dr. Brulet explained…

PLAYER #3

"They were so highly developed that it is inconceivable to think that they have simply perished."

PLAYER #3
(Continuing)
"The documents my team discovered mentioned a dream-like state the Atlantians were capable of achieving which allowed them to breathe and travel freely while underwater."

"I fully intend to prove that they still exist and that Atlantis is still a functioning and thriving undiscovered world."

PLAYER #6
The Paris-based expert is widely recognized as a leading authority on ancient and lost civilisations. She has already led several major expeditions to locate the fabled society of Atlantis. To date, all these endeavors were focused on the Atlantic Ocean.

But the fruitlessness of her Atlantic searches has now convinced her to look elsewhere. Upon proving the authenticity of the newly discovered maps, she plans to assemble a new team and look for Atlantis in the Pacific.

Or as she insisted…

PLAYER #3
"I believe we should now refer to this underwater domain as 'Pacifica'."

"My aim is to establish radio-sonar contact with the inhabitants. If they respond, we would uncover an entirely new dimension to human history."

PLAYER #6
Dr. Brulet published her findings in the scientific journal, 'Nature', last month. She confirmed the discovery of the maps and documents, but continues to guard their contents fiercely.

PLAYER #3
"I must protect what has been unearthed from buccaneers and treasure-hunters. This is not only a matter of scientific debate. It also carries an obligation to preserve a once in a life time discovery."

"This is far too important an opportunity to see it undermined by pirates."

PLAYER #6
She did, however, state in her article that the documents and maps discovered appear to be well over 5,000 years old.

Her published report went on to suggest that the inhabitants of Atlantis:

- Belong to a super-intelligent race that mastered nuclear power while ordinary humans were still hunting with spears.

- Travelled in airships thousands of years ago and may well be piloting UFOs today.

- And may have life spans of hundreds or possibly thousands of years.

Dr. Brulet stated in an interview…

PLAYER #3

"I believe that the greatest discovery, disclosed in my paper, was of the Atlantian practice of a transcendent, dream-like state referred to as 'L'Oolaloo'."

"It is this L'Oolaloo technique which has allowed them to live underwater without requiring any breathing apparatus whatsoever."

"This ability, together with their advanced architectural methods, demonstrates that they would be perfectly capable of survival even after their empire sank to the ocean floor. To find them would be the pinnacle of my career. A dream come true."

PLAYER #6

Dr. Brulet speculates the Atlantians covered their cities with clear bubble-like structures of enormous strength before Atlantis began to sink.

PLAYER #3

"These people are obviously a vastly-superior race and non-violent in nature. They have followed a strict policy of non-interference in human affairs for thousands of years."

"Now, we must try to contact them to save our planet. We need their knowledge. We must find them and it's only a matter of time before we do."

FX: Lights change for 'Psychic Calls #3'

PSYCHIC CALLS #3

PLAYERS #3, #4, #5, #6 address the audience in turn.

PLAYER #4
Order the one and only 'Lucky Irish Pixie Dream Charm'! Whatever you seek, we GUARANTEE the 'Lucky Irish Pixie Dream Charm' will work its magic for you. Don't delay! Order now!

PLAYER #5
Call our Pet Dream Psychics! Do you really know what's going on as your pet dreams? We do! For all the love your pet gives you, doesn't your pet deserve this call? Open the dream passage between you and your beloved pet. Why wait?!

PLAYER #3
Do you ever feel like someone is watching over you? Do you ever hear a voice speaking to you in your dreams? It could be your Guardian Angel! Let us put you in touch with the gentle spirit who guides you. Good fortune awaits! Special rates for our first-time callers.

PLAYER #6
Try Britain's most reliable psychic source. Our psychics' powers are well documented. Why settle for second best? Have your dreams interpreted and gain amazing insights from our gifted psychics. We are just a call away! Call now, now, now!

PLAYER #4

'Life is but a dream!' Let Lady Marcia connect you to the life your dreams reveal for you. Open your dream-life connection! Your true destiny awaits.

FX: Lights change for 'Dream Howler'
FX: Sound effect of wolves howling

DREAM HOWLER

PLAYER #7

Dreamline Madrid: 'Man Turns into a Werewolf at Planetarium Lunar Show!'

FX: Sound effect out

Madrid, Spain- Police were called to a planetarium after a member of the audience at a special lunar lights show began howling at the moon- and transformed into a werewolf!

Eyewitnesses claim that the yet to be named man, a well-dressed individual in his mid to late 30's, had to be restrained and handcuffed after he became violent and threatened other members of the audience and the police with physical harm.

Manolo Vasquez, a witness to the bizarre scene, stated…

PLAYER #4

"The lights went down, the stars and the moon were projected above us, and then this beastly baying and howling broke out."

PLAYER #4
(Continuing)
"They turned on the lights again and I saw this hombre- snarling and covered with fur. He was sitting in the seat right behind me!"

"He was a real sight. He was dressed in a suit, but otherwise he was like some wild animal with sharp teeth and pointy ears."

"He lunged at my girlfriend who was sitting next to me. I never heard such terrified screaming and crying in my life. It was a living nightmare."

"Thank God the police came when they did. We were all in danger from this beast-man."

PLAYER #7
Authorities have so far refused to identify the supposed lycanthrope's identity. He was eventually arrested after a prolonged struggle with police at the National Planetarium in Madrid.

Two members of the police force at the scene were hospitalised from their injuries. Their condition is currently unknown.

An official police report released yesterday stated that the attacker was now being held at a secure facility for the criminally insane.

There was no comment made to the public about the nature of the man's appearance.

PLAYER #7
(Continuing)
According to the police report, the man arrived at the
planetarium alone, purchased his entry ticket, and
then took his place among the other members of the
audience.

Eyewitness Vasquez, 17, a waiter at a local tapas bar,
added…

PLAYER #4
"He was quiet, pleasant-looking, and nicely dressed
in a brown serge suit. I noticed him, because he
arrived just as the show was about to begin."

"He seemed strangely familiar somehow. I saw him
shuffle past others in his row as he made his way to
his seat."

PLAYER #7
Vasquez claims that shortly after the planetarium
show began a representation of the moon appeared on
the overhead screens.

Soon, he heard a commotion behind him and the
sound of howling.

PLAYER #4
"At first, I thought someone was just horsing around."

PLAYER #7
But seconds later, when the house lights came back
on, he stated that he saw the well-dressed man in the
brown suit had undergone a shocking transformation.

PLAYER #4
"He was covered in fur, slobbering, and yelping like some rabid animal."

"I could not believe my eyes. His hands were hairy with long sharp claws. His face was no longer human. He looked like a wolf."

"And that's when it dawned on me. It's why I thought he looked familiar when I first saw him."

"I had a really disturbing dream just last week about someone turning into an animal. I woke up screaming. 'The wolf man has me, Momma! The wolf man has me!' I kept screaming until my mum told me to shut it and go back to sleep."

"This man looked just like the one I saw turn into a wolf in my dream."

"That's why I thought I recognized him when he first sat down. He was the man from my dream!"

PLAYER #7
Police reported that as the lights came back on the man stopped his howling and began snarling and intimidating the people around him. He clawed at the woman sitting next to Mr. Vasquez and soon everyone stampeded toward the exits.

The police report stated that there were several injuries to audience members trampled in the panic. Their condition however is not yet known.

PLAYER #7
(Continuing)
Newspaper, online commentary, and television news accounts set off a wave of panic in the city. Madrid authorities issued a series of announcements urging the public to remain calm and cast doubt on the accuracy of eyewitness statements.

Mr. Vasquez, however, insisted on the truth of his version of events…

PLAYER #4
"That man turned into a werewolf right in front of my eyes. I didn't dream this. Well, I did dream it. But this time it really happened."

FX: Lights change

ZOLTAR
I am Zoltar
From a far off star
Seller of dreams

I am Zoltar
From a far off star
Dealer in destiny

FX: Lights change to a blue watery state
FX: Sound effect of gentle rain

ZOLTAR
A group of strangers
A wet umbrella

ZOLTAR
(Continuing)
A mustard moustache
An ancient apple tree
We hear a heart beating
We watch someone drowning

FX: Sound effect of turbulent water rushing

All **PLAYERS**, barring **SANDMAN #1, 2**, react as if drowning in dumb show and resume their sleeping positions as when first seen by the audience.

ZOLTAR
All the things that live in dreams
Are Zoltar's to command

FX: Sound effect of water fades
FX: Blackout

PLAYERS #7, #8 exit to **Corridor Exit Area** (Section 4) in the blackout

FX: Light change

SANDMAN #1, #2 begin leading the audience out of the **Open Performance area** (Section 3) and into the **Corridor Exit Area** (Section 4).

As the audience makes their exit, **Zoltar** sings a lullaby in a language with which the audience is unlikely to find familiar.

FX: PA music
FX: Lights-**Corridor Exit Area**

33

In the **Corridor Exit Area** (Section 4), **PLAYERS #7, #8** are already in position. They sit tightly together. Their arms are draped over one another's shoulders.

SANDMAN #1, #2 direct the audience to be seated.

FX: PA music out
FX: Lights for 'Ordinary Women'

ORDINARY WOMEN

PLAYER #7
We are ordinary women.

PLAYER #8
We never thought ourselves special.

PLAYER #7
I was happy with the family.

PLAYER #8
I was happy with my life.

PLAYERS #7, #8
We are ordinary women

Player # 7
Ordinary

PLAYER #8
Yes, that's quite right.

PLAYER #7
We didn't know each other.

PLAYER #8
Not until that night

PLAYERS #7, #8
We were strangers.

PLAYER #8
Then on 23rd April 2022 at 7.35 in the evening

PLAYER #7
I remember checking the time.

PLAYER #8
At 7.35 in the evening

PLAYER #7
We saw an amazing light.

PLAYER #8
It was like a glowing bubble

PLAYER #7
It was like a crystal ball

PLAYER #8
Hovering just above us

PLAYERS #7, #8
Hovering. Then descending

PLAYER #7
It was slowly dropping down

PLAYER #8
While growing larger and larger

PLAYER #7
And slowly dropping down.

PLAYER #8
Then we looked at one another.

PLAYERS #7, #8
Me at you. You at me.

PLAYER #7
And saw ourselves identical.

PLAYER #8
Not in how we looked, but what we are.

PLAYER #7
We knew we were identical.

PLAYER #8
In a fundamental way

PLAYER #7
I believe we saw our spirit.

PLAYERS #7, #8
Me in you. You in me.

PLAYER #8
While swallowed in that light.

PLAYER #7
We simply stood there staring

PLAYER #8
We saw ourselves alive.

PLAYER #7
For the first time ever really

PLAYER #8
We saw ourselves alive.

PLAYER #7
It was more than standing naked.

PLAYER #8
We felt far more exposed.

PLAYER #7
Then as quickly as we noticed

PLAYER #8
The light began to rise.

PLAYER #7
Slowly

PLAYER #8
But higher

PLAYERS #7, #8
The light began to rise.

PLAYER #7
It hovered for a moment.

PLAYER #8
The light began to blink.

PLAYER #7
I felt my body splitting.

PLAYER #8
I was being torn in two.

PLAYER #7
I reached across to grab you.

PLAYER #8
I grabbed you.

PLAYER #7
I grabbed you.

PLAYERS #7, #8
I reached across to grab you.

PLAYER #7
When suddenly… it was gone.

PLAYER #8
We looked at one another.

PLAYERS #7, #8
Me at you. You at me.

PLAYER #7
And began to understand.

PLAYER #8
There's something of me in you.

PLAYER #7
And something in you of me.

PLAYER #8
We're a single being really.

PLAYER #7
Not two

PLAYER #8
Not two

PLAYER #7
A single being

PLAYER #8
Really

PLAYERS #7, #8
Not two

PLAYER #7
(In a sing-song manner)
♫ "I want what you want."

PLAYER #8
"I'll do what you do."

PLAYER #7
"All the things that you believe"

PLAYER #8
"I believe them too." ♫
(Sing-song manner out)

PLAYER #7
We're ordinary women

PLAYER #8
In an ordinary way

PLAYER #7
But we do nothing without the other

PLAYERS #7, #8
Night or day

PLAYER #8
We didn't know each other.

PLAYER #7
Not until that night

PLAYERS #7, #8
We were strangers.

PLAYER #7
Then on 23rd April 2022 at 7.35 in the evening

PLAYER #8
I remember she checked the time.

PLAYER #7
At 7.35 in the evening

PLAYER #8
We saw an amazing light.

PLAYER #7
It was like a glowing bubble

PLAYER #8
It was like a crystal ball

PLAYER #7
Hovering just above us

PLAYERS #7, #8
Hovering. Then descending

PLAYER #8
It was slowly dropping down

PLAYER #7
While growing larger and larger

PLAYER #8
And slowly dropping down.

PLAYER #7
Then we looked at one another

PLAYERS #7, #8
Me at you. You at me.

PLAYER #8
And saw ourselves identical

PLAYER #7
Not in how we looked, but what we are.

PLAYER #8
We knew we were identical

PLAYER #7
In a fundamental way.

PLAYER #8
I believe we saw our spirit.

PLAYERS #7, #8
Me in you. You in me.

PLAYER #7
While swallowed in that light.

PLAYER #8
We simply stood there staring

PLAYER #7
And saw ourselves alive.

PLAYER #8
For the first time ever really

PLAYER #7
We saw ourselves alive.

PLAYER #8
It was more than standing naked

PLAYER #7
We felt far more exposed.

PLAYER #8
Then as quickly as we noticed

PLAYER #7
The light began to rise.

PLAYER #8
Slowly

PLAYER #7
But higher

PLAYERS #7, #8
The light began to rise.

PLAYER #8
It hovered for a moment

PLAYER #7
The light began to blink.

PLAYER #8
I felt my body splitting.

PLAYER #7
I was being torn in two.

PLAYER #8
I reached across to grab you

PLAYER #7
I grabbed you.

PLAYER #8
I grabbed you.

PLAYERS #7, #8
I reached across to grab you

PLAYER #8
When suddenly…it was gone.

PLAYER #7
We looked at one another

PLAYERS #7, #8
Me at you. You at me.

PLAYER #8
And began to understand.

PLAYER #7
There's something of me in you.

PLAYER #8
And something in you of me.

PLAYER #7
We're a single being really

PLAYER #8
Not two

PLAYER #7
Not two

PLAYER #8
A single being

PLAYER #7
Really

PLAYERS #7, #8
Not two.

PLAYER #8
(In a sing-song manner)
♫ "I want what you want."

PLAYER #7
"I'll do what you do."

PLAYER #8
"All the things that you believe"

PLAYER #7
"I believe them too." ♫
(Sing-song manner out)

PLAYER #8
We're ordinary women

PLAYER #7
In an ordinary way

PLAYER #8
But we do nothing without the other…

PLAYERS #7, #8
Night or day.

FX: Lights change

PLAYERS #7, #8 rise, turn toward the Dreamland enclosure exit, and beckon the audience to follow them back into the Club area.

SANDMAN #1, #2 follow behind encouraging the audience toward the exit.

All **PLAYERS** regroup and prepare for next audience selection to enter the Dreamland enclose.

-END-

Additional **DREAMLAND** Content …

DARKSIDE OF THE MOON

PLAYER C
(Singing a cappella in the darkness)
♫ Fly me to the moon
Let me play among the stars
Let me see what Spring is like on
A Jupiter and Mars…♫

FX: Lights change

PLAYER A
Dreamline: Bognor Regis. 'Conspiracy Crackpot threatens Suicide over Loony Lunar Claim'

Bognor Regis, England. Police were called to a local council office after an unidentified man ascended the stairwell and threatened to jump from the roof!

Eyewitnesses claimed that the man stood there holding a placard which read, 'Hands off our Moon!'

Maurice Johnson, a spokesperson for the council stated…

PLAYER B
"How he gained access to the premises and got to the stairwell, we do not know."

PLAYER B
(Continuing)
"Somehow he slipped past our security."

"Several Council workers said they watched as he carried his sign and a loud-hailer up the stairs with him. But no one thought to stop him."

"Soon, we could all hear him shouting from the roof. He was absolutely raving. Poor chap."

PLAYER A
Council security immediately contacted police who arrived on the scene shortly thereafter. But the police were unable to gain access to the roof, because the intruder had barricaded the roof entrance.

He claimed to have wired it with explosives and the building was then promptly cleared.

PLAYER B
"We could all hear him screaming something about the moon and 'aliens' who he insisted were occupying it."

"He was clearly deeply troubled. He repeatedly vowed that he would jump, if his 'manifesto' was not broadcast by the BBC."

"People began gathering outside the building. When the man saw the large crowd staring up at him, he began reading his 'manifesto' through the loud-hailer."

PLAYER A
One of the onlookers recorded the man's rambling
manifesto and shared it with this reporter…

FX: Lights change

PLAYER C
"Can you hear me? This you need to know! I would
rather die than let alien forces take our moon from us!
Drastic matters demand drastic measures!"

"Everyone knows about Moonrocks and Moondust
and the astronauts playing their weightless lunar golf
nonsense, don't we? You all either saw it on the box
or it's in your history books."

"But did you know all this was seen and done on the
nearside of the Moon? Well, it was."

"What you don't know is that we have photographs of
the farside too. And that's a fact."

"Although no one has yet to set foot there-this is
virgin golf territory if you will-Lunar Orbiter V
completely imaged and mapped this farside region
and let me tell you something. The farside of the
Moon -the darkside- that is a different kettle of fish
altogether."

"Let me repeat that just in case your cloth ears
couldn't listen…A different kettle of fish!
Altogether!"

PLAYER C
(Continuing)
"I'm sure you don't remember this, but I do. Do you
recall, you probably don't, that the Beeb reported,
now this is true, mind, the BBC ran reports claiming
that NASA photos of the darkside of our Moon
revealed huge alien machines, several of them, over a
mile long and engaged in intelligent mining
operations?"

"Wow! Are you listening to this? Wow-wow. That's
a double wow."

"The Beeb report stated that one photograph was
particularly inexplicable. The scientist being
interviewed for her views admitted that she was
utterly baffled and could offer no explanation."

"This NASA photograph showed a huge machine, the
BBC reported this, mind, a machine working away
along the top of a huge crater and what appears to be
an enormous plume of Moondust shooting up into the
air!"

"I don't know what this means. Don't ask me. I don't
know what to believe anymore.
But if this is true-and it was widely reported as true-
if it's true, this should be investigated very carefully.
But it is not! It is ignored!"

"There's a distinct possibility that what we are
assuming is worthless Moondust, at the moment, may
be in fact a very special element or mineral that may
be in very short supply THROUGHOUT THE
UNIVERSE!"

49

"Think about it. Years from now we discover we can create something truly life-changing, if ONLY we had this one ingredient that USED to be in plentiful supply on the darkside of our very own Moon. However, when we weren't paying attention, sneaky alien miners stripped it all away!"

"This has me terrified and should terrify you too."

"This sort of thing happens all the time here on Earth. Minerals, we never thought would be of value, turn out to be the most useful of all. The world has already descended into a turf war over mineral rights that we never imagined we would require. Until now. Now, they call them 'rare earth minerals'. And there's a global fight on to get hold of them."

"Oh! How I'd like to be like the rest of you- totally unaware of the situation-but it is too late for that. I remember these reports quite clearly and for some unknown reason you seem to have forgotten all about them. It's like a collective amnesia has come upon us."

"People can be so frustrating at times. I mean, the information is out there-published reports, out there on the web. Oh! It's so frustrating!"

"We claim we want to be informed. We act like we are informed- that we are interested-we watch the news- we have opinions- and yet when some startling discovery comes to light, do we remember it?"

PLAYER C
(Continuing)
"Or do we remember only what we want to
remember? And forget the rest?"

"And so the real concerns that should weigh heavily
upon us are forgotten. We jump to the next thing and
forget the essential things of before."

"You don't remember. You can't recall. So, look it up
yourselves, if you don't believe me. It's there. 'BBC
Nationwide' broadcast these images on a drizzly
evening on 16th March 1977. 30 million viewers
tuned in-30 million-and the reports continued in
newspapers and magazines for nearly four weeks
afterward."

"But we forget. We blanked it all out for some reason.
You never told your children and so they are ignorant
too."

"I take my stand here. I lay my life down for the
planet. May my sacrifice wake us up to the truth!"

"Perhaps we are being manipulated to forget. I don't
know."

"Perhaps the aliens are already here on Earth-mining
what was once ours-and we are oblivious to the
evidence right in front of our own eyes."

"I am your alarm! Stop dreaming! I am your call to
arms. I am your church bell tolling!"

PLAYER C
(Continuing)
"If these reports are true, right now on the darkside of
our Moon, alien forces may be literally undermining
our inheritance. And we're all just ignoring it,
watching the latest tittle-tattle, self-consumed."

"Wake up! Rise up! We must not be like ostriches
with our heads in the Moondust. Our future-our
freedom- is on the line."

"Contact your MP. Form a lobbying group. Agitate
for more Moon flights to investigate further."

"Sometimes, you just have to pull your finger out and
do something. You know what I'm saying?"

"Follow me back to the Darkside of the Moon!"

(Singing)
♫ Fly me to the moon
Let me play among the stars
Let me see what Spring is like on
A Jupiter and Mars…♫

FX: Lights change

PLAYER A
Throughout his thunderous fulmination, some
onlookers below began to heckle and jeer.

Maurice Johnson, a council spokesperson stated…

PLAYER B

"It was quite alarming. Some in the mob started chanting, 'Take a moon-walk, nutter!' Scuffles broke out. This unfortunate man was deranged and some people acted as if it were the latest reality show and began actively encouraging the poor chap to jump."

"Such behaviour is completely contrary to our Council's social guidelines and the stated policy on our website which promotes inclusiveness, diversity, and community cohesion."

PLAYER A

Eventually, a BBC camera crew arrived and was allowed access to the scene.

Their reporter interviewed the man through the barricaded door and promised his 'lunar message' would be broadcast.

Police forces at the stand-off were then able to coax the man to open the roof access door and surrender himself.

His claim to have wired the roof access with explosives was revealed to be a hoax.

As the police led the man away, he continued with his rambling diatribe…

PLAYER C

"You may chain and handcuff me. You may silence me. But you will never silence the truth!"

PLAYER C
(Continuing)
"And when my story is aired, I hope that Elon Musk
chappie will be watching. He has his own rockets.
Good old Musky will figure out what those aliens are
up to. He'll figure out what those aliens are mining.
And I bet it's just the thing he needs to make his
electric cars run right."

FX: Lights-blackout

-END-

ABOUT CHARLES SERIO

Charles Serio is artistic director of Serio Ensemble.
The Ensemble focuses on new writing and
performing arts. Six of his published plays have been
produced and performed in the United Kingdom, the
European Union, and in America.

He is a former finalist in the London Writers'
Competition-poetry division and a former prize
winner of the British New Plays Competition. He
works as a professional actor, teacher, and director.

He is a previous winner of an Emmy award for his
scriptwriting on the CBS television series, *In Our
Lives*.

His first novel, *The Lies I've Told,* was published in 2015. Another of his novels, *The Legend of the Blue Cloud*, was published in 2019.

Charles also leads highly acclaimed corporate presentation skills programs internationally.

He lives in London.

www.charlesserio.com
enquiry@charlesserio.com

www.ingramcontent.com/pod-product-compliance
Lightning Source LLC
Chambersburg PA
CBHW050006070726
47592CB00018B/1065